ANTICIPATION

The door was open. Jan waited for me, leaning on the mantel above the fireplace, firelight hinting along the contours where his shirt and pants followed the forms of his body. He watched me approach, his head cocked to one side. I came within the direct look of those misty eyes, and there was nothing but those eyes. We kissed. After a long time he pulled my head back gently and, with both hands, looked at me—questioning looks at my cheeks, my lips. "You look like a hungry baby bird," he laughed. I had his clothes off in no time, and we fell to the floor before the fire.

Avon Books are available at special quantity discounts for bulk purchases for sales promotions, premiums, fund raising or educational use. Special books, or book excerpts, can also be created to fit specific needs.

For details write or telephone the office of the Director of Special Markets, Avon Books, 959 8th Avenue, New York, New York 10019, 212-262-3361.

MY BROTHER'S IMAGE

MARK HAMILTON

NOT ADDED BY UNIVERSITY OF MICHIGAN

AVON
PUBLISHERS OF BARD, CAMELOT, DISCUS AND FLARE BOOKS

MY BROTHER'S IMAGE is an original publication of Avon Books.
This work has never before appeared in book form.

AVON BOOKS
A division of
The Hearst Corporation
959 Eighth Avenue
New York, New York 10019

Copyright © 1983 by Mark Hamilton
Published by arrangement with the author
Library of Congress Catalog Card Number: 82-90519
ISBN: 0-380-82230-x

All rights reserved, which includes the right to
reproduce this book or portions thereof in any form
whatsoever except as provided by the U. S. Copyright Law.
For information address Avon Books.

First Avon Printing, February, 1983

AVON TRADEMARK REG. U.S. PAT. OFF. AND IN
OTHER COUNTRIES, MARCA REGISTRADA, HECHO EN
U. S. A.

Printed in the U. S. A.

WFH 10 9 8 7 6 5 4 3 2 1

For my father
Sam Hamilton

CHAPTER ONE

I AM EIGHTEEN. Centuries ago, when I was a child, I think I knew more than I know now. The disposition toward adventure and the sweet and threatening smile of beauty were near me then like ghosts of my future. Tender ghosts they were, hovering near me when I dreamed or said good-bye; frightened ghosts, lost in love and hiding their wounds from me behind the vibrant curtain that surrounds a child's life. And when, approaching the time of sex, I dreamed of having life—of putting my arms around the sinuous, wild unknown—I think the ghosts of my future sighed, thrashing among one another, calling to me in airy, lost voices: "Do not hurry! Stay a boy as long as you can." But, as with all forbidden things, the future seduced me by resisting me. Beauty, I knew, waited by the turning of the road, and would lie down with me.

I was a lover from the first, never at peace, excited. Our Dutch landscapes; fields riven only by the gentlest rises of earth along the canals, the order of flowers, windmills, hayricks, under which dwelt the deepest of mysteries. We prospered. I was a landowner among landowners in the Netherlands in the Year of Grace 1729. The breath of God throbbed in my family's lands as if that pulse were, after all, companionable. Help me decide, as I tell you this, what lay there.

I am Steen van Leuwen. My twin brother's name is Moenen. When we played hide-and-seek in the fields I did not search for Moenen. I was chasing life. Moenen hid.

I must tell you about us, about a day in summer like summers you remember; childhood, when things are so large and the colors come to you as if they were secrets blown on winds. Moenen and I were twelve, playing in a field of grass near our family's country house. Two blond boys, our own secrets the more intriguing for being so well known to each other. The hedges along the canal that bordered the field were cut into animal shapes. There was a partridge, a dog pawing at the air with leafy paws, a horse's rearing head and hooves. There were fantastical animals, too. These drew me; a dragon with exquisitely long wings above the hedge, an elephant's long trunk. I stood under the dragon's wings while Moenen hid, and when I looked up I know I was expecting to see the veins of a real live dragon's wing. The leafy edges somehow never compromised that vision. The shade smelled of dragon. Maybe there were dragon's eggs nearby, you see.

I would go looking for my brother, and if he was nowhere, I always returned to his favorite place, down the little bank of the canal, under the wooden bridge. That one day Moenen did not know he was discovered. I found him rapt in contemplation of the supporting rafters of the bridge. There was a curious motion in the darkness. I remember Moenen as he stood; so deep was his concentration that I felt it immediately. His little leather belt hung only half buckled, and one pant leg remained rolled to his knee, while the other had fallen back down to his ankle. He heard me rustle through the tall grass, and he pointed to a large, white seabird with a hooked beak that had gotten caught among the bridge rafters. One wing was wedged into an angle where a support joined a beam. Doves often nested there; perhaps this bird had been eating their eggs. Moenen was up among the rafters in an instant, freeing the bird easily. It was almost larger than he was, and it cut him. There was blood on his cheek as he reached the ground and began dragging it up the bank.

Just as we got to the top there was a tremendous clattering of hooves coming across the bridge toward us. It was as if a giant horseman had come out of nowhere. The dust swirled around us as we saw the red rider, crimson cape billowing behind him. His horse's sweat and spittle sprayed us. I remember the jingling and clanking of the tackle, and the tiny explosions of blood where the rider's spurs dug into the chestnut skin. The bird took fright, beating its wings, flying up so that the great figure had to flex his whip arm to bat the bird out of the way. Moenen gripped his bird's feet. As I watched the red rider billowing down the road, Moenen struggled with the bird in the dust beside me, crying in his high-pitched, child's voice, "Whoa, whoa." Then the bird made a good, concentrated effort to fly, and the two of them were off down the line of the canal, toward a stand of poplar trees on our estate.

The poplars ring a beautiful, still pond, a millpond without a mill beside it. The trees are tall, ageless, of a green so deep it is almost black-green. Already, in those years, we loved the poplar copse.

When I found them, Moenen had secured the bird to a sapling, his belt around its neck. It struggled wildly, and its beak had cut his shoulders in several places, but the bird was not going anywhere. My brother was busy weaving little pine boughs among larger branches fallen from the poplars.

Moenen looked up at me just as a beam of sunlight cut through the trees above us, crossing his face with a radiance of church-window gold. His blue eyes sparkled. "Help me," he called, and said he was making the bird a shelter. My brother and I held hands. Four tiny hands. He looked into my face. Blood was still wet on his hands and dripped a little from the cuts on his cheek. I said the bird already belonged to someone. "Who?" he asked. "God," I said. He cocked his head and smiled at me in a way I have since learned to call "indulgent," and said I was silly.

"It is mine," he said. "I found it and tamed it." Although his tone was a fighting tone, he held my hands gently.

I remember feeling quite urgent about the bird's freedom and I argued with him about it. When I described how the bird would starve, I convinced him. It was a wild bird. My brother thought hard. He looked at the reflections on the pond while the white bird thrashed in the brush beside us, its fury framing our silence. Moenen was thinking, with the sunlight sparkling in his eyes, how the world was full of sudden riders of all kinds, red riders. Moenen was straining, like the bird. As he gazed at the pond, I stroked his foot once, and he turned to the white commotion. As he grasped the bird by the neck, bending over it, his hair mingled with the white feathers, and while the bird struggled, my brother wiped his wounds, one by one, across the feathers of the bird's back, smearing his blood there. Then he looked at me and we began to struggle with the bird, each catching one of the wings at its base. We carried the thrashing creature to the edge of the silent pond, where images of poplars lay on the water. We caught the bird by the lower body and threw it into the air. It struggled toward the water, then found steady flight, crying angrily. As it circled in the air above us, I could still see Moenen's crimson chevrons on its back. Moenen shouted to the bird, "You tell Him, tell Him you belong to me now. Show Him my blood!"

I held my brother's hand until the bird was out of sight in the deep summer sky.

I cannot give you much of a foretaste of doom in describing our childhood. We were prosperous and carefree. Our father died when we were very little, leaving us estates, a fortune, and our house in Amsterdam. Our mother had a broad forehead, deep dark eyes, and dark hair. Mother was interested in things. She was a patron of the arts, especially painting; painters came and went through our city house, sometimes working in rooms my mother encouraged them to use because of the fine quality of the light from the great windows. I remember once she had a holy man from the Indies to visit. He wore a turban and white, flowing robes. He had been brought to Amsterdam by one of our princes, and mother persuaded him to extend his visit by staying several days in our house. She was like that, as once when she bent her large frame over a watchmaker's working table, her dark braids brushing the table, and asked the man minute questions about his craft. So, it seemed, did she bend over the little Hindu in our parlor. He sat cross-legged on a Persian rug, and she served him tea.

I supposed he was a saint of some kind. He had a white beard and deep creases in his face and perfect white teeth. His eyes danced. Once I encountered him standing in the hall outside his room holding an object toward me. He had unpacked a present for me, it seemed: a giant conch shell. As he held it, he was offering me the whole world, cradling the globe of Earth, smiling. The reds and pinks of the conch shell played around his eyes. I remember a feeling of great love when he gave me that shell.

My mother did not invite people in to show off this guest. She had him for us alone, and for those friends who always visited. The saint spent part of his days watching a painter who was working under our roof and whose last name was the same as my given one—Steen. He was the grandson of the famous Steen. The swami loved to watch this Steen work, sometimes standing just behind him. The swami's presence was so gentle that he was not a disturbance, and his only reaction to the painter's work was an occasional giggle. One day when I, too, was watching I saw Steen line the highlight on a church steeple in a country scene, and as the brushstroke gave it light, the swami made a delighted little giggle. A smile crossed my lips. And Steen's.

Mother did not attempt to converse much with the swami, though he spoke an adequate Dutch, having learned it from our colonists in his country. She communicated with him by an ability she had with gestures. Once she pared an apple, then sliced it and gave him the first section. There was a fine understanding in their eyes, a solemnity, and he put his hand on her forehead and blessed her.

On the last night of his visit I encountered the swami unexpectedly, long after everyone else was in bed. I was sixteen that winter and I had a habit of wakefulness. When I woke in the dark I would wander the house in an overcoat until I felt sleepy again. Moenen never woke with me, though often when I left our room he would stir in his bed. I went silently down the staircase and into the gallery, where tall French doors gave a view of the terrace, the garden, and the canal beyond. I gazed out through the glass doors; my feeling in the dark hours of those childhood mornings was of the richness of the sleeping world. Sometimes I danced around and around, humming to the furniture. Waiting.

Far at the end of the gallery, through the door to the glass room, a candle glimmered. It was January, and the little room was bare of its plants. A rounded conservatory with walls and roof of glass, it was usually kept closed through winter because it got so cold. Seeing the candle, I wondered who was enduring the cold room at that dark hour. I slid silently across the gallery floor to find out, and when I pushed the door open, I discovered the swami, wearing only a loincloth, meditating before his candle. The whole night sky sparkled through the glass walls and roof behind him. Very slowly, he opened his eyes. Candlelight danced on his cheeks, in his irises, as he focused on me sitting wrapped in my coat.

A chunk of dry, powdery snow dropped to the window-roof from the eaves, and I looked up, startled by the noise in the stillness. When I glanced back at him, the swami was regarding me with great concentration. One of his hands was motionless on his knee. The other twirled a sprig of evergreen with red berries on it, tiny red berries with holes in one end. Beyond his shoulders the constellations twinkled in the blue dark; the candle made a warmth between us. His gaze was not disconcerting; it was comforting. I was not embarrassed; I looked back at him.

Some of what follows is verbatim, and I keenly remember the sense of it all. He glanced from me to the evergreen sprig he was twirling, then back to me, and occasionally to a place above my head. Finally his eyes came fully into mine, and he said, "When did you stop drinking milk?"

"Last year." I think I cradled my head in my palms.

"If you ever want to sleep uninterrupted, you need only drink a large glass of milk before you sleep. Warm or not, it doesn't matter."

"Thank you. But I enjoy being up."

"For then you walk on the world with many legs," he said.

We smiled. He asked, "Has it never occurred to you how much more you see than other children see?"

I said not. He asked, "To whom do you make love?"

"My brother. But not for a long time now."

The swami said, "You will have many lovers, but not he."

"Will he die?"

"That is not the reason," he said.

"Will I know women?"

MY BROTHER'S IMAGE

"Yes, but more men, I think. Be careful not to masturbate too much. It disuses you for other pleasures."

"Tell my fortune." I drew my coat around me tightly.

"You will know God." He held the evergreen sprig in the candle flame a moment, but it did not burn.

"Where will I meet Him?"

"You are a beautiful boy. You would fetch a king's ransom in my country."

"Where will I meet Him?"

"In the ruins."

"Will our houses fall down?"

"Whatever happens, remember I told you that you will never be crushed. Remember this sign," he said, and he tossed the sprig of evergreen into the air. It hung above our heads, suspended, catching the candlelight while I watched. After a few moments, he put out the candle with two fingers and I heard the evergreen drop onto the floor. The swami picked it up and touched my forehead with it, then placed it in my hand, telling me to go and sleep. I left his shape there beneath the winter sky, and as I climbed the stairs I already had begun to wonder if what I had seen could really have happened. The berries from that evergreen are in a little silver box I have.

You may see me as a boy, in a very small painting by Steen. He modeled me soon after the swami had left us, and I suppose Steen picked me because our names are the same. The tiny painting is of a farm family at prayer before the evening meal. A cow looks in through a door at the rear; the light is that of a serene, early evening in summer. A father, mother, and little girl stand at the table with their hands folded and their little heads bowed, but the boy of the family, though his hands are folded, is not praying with the others. He is gazing straight out of the small frame with an open, frank curiosity into your eyes, as if trying to catch the attention of the painter. I think it is the most intimate moment I have ever seen on a canvas.

With portraits enough of us, I suppose, that was not a picture my mother wished to buy, but we did have a party to celebrate its completion. There were some painters, a few other burgher families, and a musician playing my mother's clavier—though with my mother, you never knew whether the musician was a friend or had been hired for the occasion. Perhaps both. The famous van Seekt was invited, and his daughter. He was a huge, flamboyant man, a walking Christmas tree, and a patron—like my mother—of painters in our city. His white hair was a halo about his shining, round face. If he hadn't been so corpulent, the effect would have been beatific.

My mother was the only matron in Amsterdam who received Seekt socially, though his various businesses provided him with highly placed contacts all over Europe, some remarkably highly placed. Seekt's fortunes were of an uncertain origin, and his way of living was rumored to be too eccentric for any good Dutch Reformed Calvinist to countenance. But my mother delighted in Seekt and in his intimate stories about princes and princesses at the courts. Where Seekt was, there generally was laughter. His wife had died after the birth of their daughter, a girl some years my senior. Even among children of the rich, who in some ways grow up so quickly, she had a reputation for sophistication acquired at the French court. Her beauty was a native Dutch effect, and she was famous for it, too.

Ten families were invited to visit that day, so there were many children, perhaps fifty people altogether. A riot of talking, coming and going through our public rooms, wealthy burghers in rich, deeply colored fabrics, their laces and jewels and the laces on their children sprinkling our halls under the chandeliers.

Steen's painting was set on an easel in the long gallery where the wall of French doors made light upon the black and white marble squares. The clavier had also been placed in that room. Just before the first carriage had halted in the drive, I slipped into the gallery to have a last look at the picture. I stopped at the double doors, however, and retreated into the hall because of what I had seen. Near the door to the hall the clavier player was bending over the instrument, tuning, and as he twisted the pegs, stray wisps of white hair from his unkempt French wig entangled themselves among the strings. Against the giant glass doors along the other wall echoed the twanging sound of a string being twisted ever sharper. Far down the gallery, against the doors to the glass room, the painting stood before a blue velvet hanging. But it was the figure in the middle distance that made me turn away. It was Moenen, who had positioned himself by the glass doors. My brother was wearing a suit of ice-blue silk; he wore white hose and lace at his neck. He stood quite stiffly, hands crossed behind his back, waiting for the guests like a monarch in a throne room. His gaze was so abstracted that I don't know whether he saw me or not. It was the first time I remembered feeling different from my brother.

Soon our hall was thronged; little children chased one another among the legs of parents and servants and tables. Burghers and their wives laughed loudly, drinking punch, embracing, discussing the foibles of relatives engaged in government or finance or love affairs. The young men and women paired off more than the older people did, or stood in groups and discussed the follies of their parents. Nothing is more haughty than a teenaged squire, or more upright. Our family had the jump on the others in that category, though, in the person of Moenen, who was greeting people in the gallery. I must mention that one of my tall male cousins came dressed in a bear suit, and, from a distance, looked quite realistically like a bear.

Seekt and his party arrived last. His clothes were more garish than anybody else's, and more obvious because of that huge frame. He combined the latest fashions from abroad, an enormous French feathered hat, with some quite out-of-date devices like knee boots and a long sword at his side. He wore an overcoat entirely of sable, large enough for two normal-sized men. My mother greeted him after pausing beside me to ask that I pay special attention to Seekt's daughter, Katje. That was thrilling. Katje was wearing a black dress, just pure black against the rich blond of her hair. That was what I liked, her simple black dress, no lace, against the forceful beauty of her unassuming countenance and bearing. She dared you not to be smitten. Not at all self-conscious, she was indulgent and respectful toward her eccentric father, who very loudly accosted my mother with fanciful titles. "My princess of the Lowlands," stamping his feet, scattering snow. Katje helped him off with his coat. My mother, holding his hat, beamed as if displaying a national treasure.

As I approached, I heard Seekt telling my mother that he had also brought along with him two "children of nature." He introduced a brother and sister. They were idiot children, each nicely dressed in silks, with faces bearing a stamp more pure than normal faces. The girl was much younger than her brother, who stood at my height. They did not drool, were not slack-jawed. What distinguished them was a certain vacant expression. No veils of doubt crossed their faces, no lines of concentration formed at eyebrows or mouths when they regarded something. As they were introduced to my mother, they seemed to comprehend that she was a person they were being made to meet, but they lacked all the tiny defensive posturings of eyes and face that people have on meeting a stranger. As each of them took it all in, the air around them felt more energetic, less predictable than it did around other people. When they spoke, their tones were as guileless as their eyes. The boy took his sister's hand, which she held up to him, and said, "We are glad to *meet* you." He looked at my mother for such a long time that I believed he meant what he said. Half his mouth twisted into a smile. He bent to his sister's ear, and her curls shook as she made a tense, prolonged curtsy, he helping her to balance on his arm.

My mother led them to the buffet table, and when the little girl beheld the roast pig with a pear in its mouth she turned back, still grasping my mother's hand, and called, "Seekt!" He walked to her across the room, which had fallen silent by then, looking at her as if deep in thought, head cocked to one side. He and my mother filled the children's plates, while I took Katje to see the painting and to meet Moenen. She liked the picture, all right, but declined to enter the large group of young people ringed around my brother, listening to him. I saw that she was, rather than shy, simply too careful to want to encounter people randomly. Her manner said, I will meet whom I want to meet, but under the right circumstances. As we glided away, she whispered in my ear, "The face in the painting is yours, not your brother's."

Leaving the gallery, I saw my brother greet a new acquaintance of his, the Spanish cardinal. The Roman see of Amsterdam had remained in the Spanish gift long after

Spain's occupation of our lands had ended. The Spanish cardinal made his majestic way across the gallery, red heels clicking on the tiles, voluminous red silk robes whispering. My brother kissed his hand. They had met the previous summer at Mayor Vilbris's council, where the cardinal was a financial adviser. My brother had gone to deliver the mayor a message from our mother, and had then stayed, captivated by the cardinal's quick wit and, I suppose, by his flattery. All that summer their strange acquaintance grew. When, one night, my mother and I declined to attend a large costume ball given by her friend Governor Iselin, Moenen went with the cardinal. As my brother bent over his hand, the cardinal's haughty, angular face, the small sharp eyes and sardonic smile, surveyed the gallery. Had it not been for the crimson skullcap on his long, straight silver-white hair, he might have looked like a mortgage appraiser staring at our rooms.

Katje and I sat on the staircase to eat supper. I positioned myself so that any view I saw included her blond hair and bare shoulders. As we ate, she told me a terrible story about events in the Hague the week before. She had been alone there in Scekt's carriage when they were stopped at the entrance to a great square. A loud and violent mob had collected, and were cheering. A whip crack was heard. Katje saw that they had tied a man's arms and legs to four horses, which were pulling him apart. She was just in time to see the joints sever, and the man's torso float in the air an instant, raining blood, before it fell to the cobblestones. Katje excused herself for telling this tale during our supper. She said that the man was Minister de Witt, the former head of government and regent for the House of Orange. The crowd was displeased by his naval policy of the previous decade, which had produced a great deal of unemployment. "Risky business, a public career in the Netherlands," I said, paraphrasing weakly a line of Cicero's. "Better warn your brother," Katje observed, licking a finger clean.

Mother was leading the little idiot girl past us up the stairs. They were saying a rhyme together, except that the girl was droning nonsense syllables. The girl steadied herself on my shoulder as they passed, as if I were a wooden banister. I looked into her great open eyes as she droned past me, struggling up the stairs, and I swore that what I saw in those eyes was tenderness. Katje explained that her father had saved them from a farm in the country, where such children are often abused, and was taking them to an orphanage he had founded at Halle. Overhead I heard the old nursery door open and soon the rocking chair began to squeak.

As we walked through the dining room, we saw Seekt engaged in conversation with the painter Steen. It looked serious enough to justify Katje's guess that her father was buying my picture. In fact, the transaction took place a few days later. We proceeded toward a growing commotion in the gallery, where we saw the bear in the midst of the young people and children. All were circling the bear, moving in to knock him on the head or snout, then darting away again before he could catch them with his bulky paws. He lumbered around the inside of the circle, grabbing at a tormentor, missing, staggering amid the wild laughter of good Dutch children. I wondered why my cousin was putting up with the hazing, but then he himself appeared out of the crowd and told me he'd gotten the idiot boy to wear the bear suit. Katje ran to fetch Seekt. I stood, watching the bear arms pawing the air in really a very bearlike way as the children smacked him. Then I had an idea. I walked, as formally as I could manage, right into the brawl. Cousins, laughing, bowed. The bear stumbled toward me and I took his arms. Inside the bear head, behind the eyeholes, the boy's ragged breaths changed to little delighted cooing sounds, delighted because someone at last had accepted his embrace. We began to dance, a slow dance with simple steps. The bear stumbled along in time, his head wagging to the rhythm. Seekt made his majestic way through the crowd, patting each child on the head, beaming and purposeful. He came and hugged us both and then removed the bear head, holding it out for the boy to hold. The boy's face and hair were drenched in sweat. He tucked the shaggy bear head under his arm.

Seekt whispered in the boy's ear and the boy nodded. I heard him say, "I will." Then Seekt turned to us, motioned for silence, and made his way to me and Katje as the boy began to sing. Though he was a big boy, his singing voice had not yet grown deep. His high, pure song told about a wolf and a lamb. At the end, the wolf eats the lamb. It was a humorous song, though no one was laughing. Beside me my mother held the little girl's hand. All the chandeliers in the gallery reflected in the girl's eyes. When the boy finished his song, he dropped the bear head onto the tiles and clapped his paws, laughing silently. We all clapped, too.

That winter was the first in my life to have a line, a series of events connected by my own responses to them. I was dancing as before a dark mirror, the dawn coming up, waiting for partners in the growing light. Katje was my big event of the season, though more so in the breach than by her presence. I saw her on only a few more occasions, occasions all centered on the idiot boy.

By the time the bear suit was removed he was shivering, and we decided to keep him at our house so he needn't be exposed to a cold ride home. Later that evening, when I looked in on him, he was very hot with fever. My mother sent for our own doctor. I changed the compresses on his forehead and stayed with him. I had felt good and useful when I saved him from his tormentors downstairs and I hoped Katje might hear of what I was doing and like me for it. I gave him the herbal potions the doctor left and stayed in his room all night. I slept, off and on, sitting up by his bed and holding his hand. I woke at dawn, a weak, purple and gray light lacing the windows and the mirrors, giving the dimensions of the room a furtive vagueness. A nightlike darkness still clung in the corners and under the furniture. All was utterly silent with the dead, ringing silence of early morning. The boy was awake, staring into my face, his eyes bright with fever. Both his hands clutched the blanket on his neck. He was still shivering, and suddenly I was afraid for him. He made small moaning noises as he pulled my hand, then grasped my head, drawing my face near to his. His bright eyes, sweat in drops along his eyebrows, the defenseless disarray of his hair after a night's fever. His voice, tight with heat and exhaustion, whispered, "I *like* dancing."

Katje came later that morning. We watched the boy sleep. My heart raced when she drew me to her. She hugged me. I looked up at her face, afraid and hoping that I might have to pretend I knew how to kiss a girl, but she was only hugging. I hugged back, and then she released me. I was confused. I had wanted so much to kiss. Katje went off to visit her friend, the daughter of Mayor Vilbris. I resolved that I would bribe one of the servants in Seekt's house so that whenever Katje was to visit us he would ride to me in time so that I could bathe before her arrival. I wondered if she had found me offensive, whether my breath was bad.

While the boy slept, I paced his room. I considered that I was in love; I wanted to ride the back of her coach, just walk or sit with her no matter what she was doing. My tutors had given me Mme. de LaFayette's novel, and when I read it I thought how empty it was. And the plays I had read or seen. When He says She has the beauty of a spring rain or of the stars on a winter midnight, I'd thought, why not simply have the midnight or the rain if you feel that way? I'd had no idea of how one's own being could become excited and enriched by another person, and there I was pacing the room and feeling more alive because Katje was in Amsterdam. Oh, I thought, no one ever made legends of love at age sixteen, yet how I pulsed for her. I looked at the winter trees, the iced canal, and I felt that that moment, and my passion, would live forever somewhere, like the boy's pure, high-voiced song echoing through the sky from star to star. Someone should *know* of this. Someone should know.

I left the sleeping boy with a servant for long enough to bathe, dressing afterward in an orange-brown velvet suit in case Katje should return that evening. Back in the sickroom I found the doctors consulting with my mother. Not even when speaking to her did they remove their wide-brimmed black hats, and I was offended. They said the boy was weak, having likely had but a poor diet all his life, and was not fighting the fever as he should. When I announced that I was nursing him, they were concerned. My mother asked what precautions I must take for myself, and the doctors said I was probably safe, but directed that a servant, not I, be the one to remove the bedpan. And, just in case, they gave me a gauze mask to wear over my nose and mouth so that no debilitating humors would enter my body. I think my mother was proud of me. The doctors bowed to me as they left the room: broad, low bows during which their hats swept the floor. So that is what it accomplishes to be finely attired and a male, I thought as I put the gauze, with its little white strings at the corners, in my pocket.

I paced the room that evening, waiting for the boy to wake, thinking of Katje and feeling as though the walls were tumbling down just out of my sight. Moenen brought me dinner on a tray, and stood watching me as I ate.

"What are you doing here?" he asked.

"Nursing."

"I don't understand."

"Have you no curiosity?" I asked.

"Nursing is for servants. This is a mere farm boy," Moenen said.

Now, a temperament like Moenen's has to be humored if one is to avoid ugly scenes. So I said, "I am going to have him for my own footman, and I want to see that he recovers. Have some lamb?"

"What are you wearing that suit for? Is the regent coming by to help you with your sisterly duties?"

That made me sad, for he'd reminded me that Katje had not come again. So Moenen got his squabble after all. "Oh, brother," I said, "I knew you would come by and supervise for at least a while, and one doesn't wear just anything to greet the ruling classes."

Somehow, this mollified him. He struck a pose which was, of course, quite lovely in a strictly visual sense. "I don't suppose," he said, "you could come out ice skating with me? You wouldn't want to leave your sisterly duties for a minute for some skating, would you?"

In the candlelight his long blond curls framed a face pretty enough to be a girl's face. Was this my face? How would someone feel, kissing those lips? "No, stop it Moenen. You come back and see me after skating, will you?"

"I wouldn't intrude," said royal Moenen, actually stomping out of the room, letting the heavy door slam solidly. My poor brother. I breathed deeply, slowly, for a few minutes. Even Moenen's new hardness was acceptable to me in that things were seeming so much more alive that winter. Katje, my sympathy for Seekt's wards, my courage in the gallery the previous day. Life was really life at last. I lost myself dreaming on the sharp, clear shapes of ice on the window, composing speeches, dozing.

I awoke fully, realizing that the room was far too warm. I was sweating, and feared for an instant that I had fallen ill. Then I saw steam coming from the ceramic stove. It had overheated. I rearranged the coals inside and banked the flame. After I had undressed, as I was putting on a thick robe for the night, I felt hands touching my back and sides. I turned around. The boy was awake, reaching, stroking my forearms. He was not perspiring, but I could feel that he was as hot as the stove. His eyes, very bright, seemed to regard me from far, far away. Perfectly silent, he took one of my hands and brought it to his mouth. He rubbed his lips across the back of my hand. I held his face then, and put my cheek to his. His cheek was so alarmingly hot! Our eyes closed, just like that for a minute. Then, in his singsong voice, congested, almost inaudible, he said, "Into the root cellar with *him*." I kissed his cheek as my robe fell to the floor and I lay on top of him, my hands holding his neck, my face to his. Even with the covers off, the heat of his body almost scorched me. I stroked his hair; he was making a frightened, shivering noise, looking past me at the ceiling. Then he said, "My friend," and his body arched, stiffened, into me. As soon as I felt his erection against my stomach, I had an orgasm, throbbing as if I were trying to fuse my flesh with his. When I recovered, I saw that his face was rigid, his eyes retreated, fixed. As I raised myself above him he remained tensed, arched; and the breath rattled out of his throat with a horrible, congested choking. Only as a bubble of blood popped on his lips did his cock spurt over his stomach and chest, white, helpless liquid shapes splashing on his flesh where the heart had ceased to beat.

I tried to lay his body back flat on the bed, but the muscles and spine had locked in an arch. I was crying, deafened by silence, as I pulled the covers over him. I left our sperm there on his body. Someone should know.

I did not run through the house like Ophelia. After I had covered him, I dressed in my irreproachable suit. It was very quiet. I went down the stairs to the gallery. Moonlight trellised the mirrors. Far down the tiles, the glass room sparkled where the door stood ajar a little. I slept against the mirrored wall.

As soon as I could manage it, I rode in my rumpled suit to Seekt's house. That morning he was sitting in a bright room with a bow window, the walls painted yellow. He looked like a great haloed whale basking in a chair. When he heard the news his chin dropped the tiny distance to his round chest and he stared at the floor.

"Maybe I should stop fussing with things," he said. I had told him no particulars. I couldn't. I had to, but I didn't. I tried to tell him what had happened to me, tell him without the facts.

He breathed hard for a while, blowing out his lower lip. "You are a prince. A merchant prince. They will seek to borrow from you someday. The crowned ones. See how expensive an initiation into life the initiation of a prince is? My sympathy is with you, my boy." Blowing his lip. It was all right; I had only come to escape Moenen, and to see Katje. And I knew he meant that, about his sympathy. When Katje came in, she had skates. At the sight of the skates my heart sank; I had none. So I couldn't confide in her. She kissed her father. I stood up, in my rumpled suit. She kissed me, and ran out again before I could speak.

I took Seekt's hand a moment and then ran from the room. I was riding out of the stables before much time had gone by, but Seekt beat me to it. As I started cantering in the court, I saw Seekt on his stairs lifting his great feathered hat to me. I reined, jerking the horse hard left to fix Seekt's salute in my vision. When our eyes met I found that I was crying, the sort of crying in which the mouth distorts. Seekt closed his eyes, lowered his head. I whipped, reined, and the horse crashed out of the courtyard, I blind.

I rode the whole day. The wounds of solitude are often the purlieu of the adolescent. Is it because people are afraid to meddle with him?

Not too many days later I heard Katje's ironic, indulgent laughter as I passed my mother's music room. They were bending over a portrait of the mayor that my mother had ordered as a gift for his birthday. That morning it was made plain to me, almost legally, if there is a legalism of the emotions, that Katje was years older and worlds more grown up than I. We walked in the frozen garden by the canal, and Katje told me about a beau she had at King Louis's court. A viscomte. Facts and descriptions escaped me. I missed the sense of some of her anecdotes, so dazed was I with my own poor confusions and with Katje's new distance from me. Oh, God, I wanted just then to have had a princess for a lover, a great princess whom Katje envied for her beauty and fame, so I could tell Katje about it.

Things have come between, but I have not tired of what happened next in that garden. My memory telescopes back down in darkness to that occasion, with no fear that the details will have changed or that I will have forgotten a thing. I recall how, in our winter clothes, under a grimacing gargoyle, the sun just breaking, she drew me into her arms and chuckled, her eyes undressing mine. She kissed me. Almost laughing, she pushed me away, my lips still open for her, smiling at me with the amusement of a painter holding up a watercolor. Then she pulled me to her and we kissed again. She chuckled.

"Steen, you are too sensual for Amsterdam. What are we going to do with you?"

I had no answer.

"You need schooling."

"I have tutors."

"Different kind of thing. Here's what I want you to do. You know, behind my father's house is the quarters for our great family's various dependents, our retainers. Whoever Daddy is interested in stays there. I want you to visit there someday soon. And write to me in France about what you find. Do you promise?"

"I do."

"Go to quarters and ask for Jan. Say I sent you."

"Will you write back?"

"And I'll see you next time I'm home," she said, buttoning my coat, shaking her rich blond hair into the wind. Then she looked at me and we were both embarrassed, thinking of something to say.

"Don't catch the French disease, now," I said. It was the wrong thing. She laughed, and walked around the side of the house to her carriage, black cloak billowing an instant among the bare hedges at the red brick corner. She disappeared into the carriage. I threw back my head to breathe and saw puffs of snow bursting in the wind from the gargoyle's paws and from his gaping, reptilian mouth. Moenen entered the garden gate from the canal, skates over his shoulder. Across the distance of the frozen winter garden, Moenen and I stared at each other while the wind blew.

CHAPTER TWO

SOME THINGS you remember. I have made a game of it, in this way: one summer morning I stood on a balcony looking over a rose garden in which Katje walked, wearing a long white dress. We had been at a party the night before and had returned to her house before I rode the rest of the way home. I was drinking a white German wine for breakfast, a glass of it sparkling in the sunlight that summer morning. I remember noting the quality of the sun. It was quite early, and the summer just bloomed. Moisture on the tips of flowers. The light was an airy breath, with not a shadow anywhere to be seen. I drank deeply. And then I saw, in perfect silence in the onionskin light, the tall blond girl in her white dress move down a lane of rosebushes. Raising her arm, she ran her finger along a thorn. I said to myself, Remember this. When you are older you will want a key by which to remember what it was to be young.

Odd moments—you cannot live with that kind of inspiration operating all the time or life would be too painful. I occasionally select moments, therefore, and say to myself, When you are in the country next summer and you look at the tops of the poplar trees, remember this pearl-drop hatpin. If you want to know in your heart the quality of winter light, remember this pearl-drop hatpin on this white marble windowsill beneath the frosted glass. I have been intentional about it.

I remember the morning, soon after my encounter with Katje, when I rode to Seekt's city house to meet the mythical Jan. Whoever Jan was, whatever she was like, I was determined that she couldn't hold a candle to Katje.

Yet Katje had spoken of her in relation to my "schooling," a more exciting than academic kind of schooling, it seemed, and so I was agitated. I had a sense, too, of watching myself—the character is on an adventure. What fun he is going to have! As I rode down the avenue that borders the canal, I slowed for a while behind a man who was driving two oxen. He used his long leather whip only to prod them occasionally; I had plenty of time to observe how sweat had frozen on the tufts of hair at the ends of their tails, which nearly dragged on the ground, and how raw and red were the insides of their flanks. I used the interval to affix to my hat a hothouse tulip I had brought with me. After all, I was going courting; the ostentation would pass unnoticed in the street as soon as I picked up speed again.

Just as the oxen turned aside, a girl with a baby in her arms rushed at me from one of the alleys where the poor live. I saw her leave a man who had a bottle to his lips, and I knew they were gin drinkers. She butted her body into my horse's chest, baby held in both arms, suckling; she held its head with her left hand. I wondered that the baby was not injured by the collision with my horse, but it made no sound as she lurched around and grabbed my stirrup. I reined in, looking down at them. She was pretty, but her hair was stringy and her face too thin; the bones were prominent. She had but the meagerest clothing, only a woolen shawl around her shoulders, a nightdress, bare feet in wooden shoes. She asked for money. I reached her down a coin, and when she put it into her bosom her hand came away from the baby's head. I saw then by the blotchy, swollen skin and upturned eyes that the baby was dead. She quickly covered it again and ran back to her man in the shadows of the ancient timbered garrets.

A fast ride over the remaining two miles to Seekt's house. That was my way, in those days, of clearing my head, riding fast as hell, letting the winter wind burn my spirit clean. I clattered into Seekt's courtyard. My horse's skin steamed. I didn't ask for Seekt; I asked Matt, the ostler, where I could find Jan, meaning to give the impression that I knew her. Matt's answer was a jerk of the head toward the upper story of the building. I climbed a winding staircase, a circular stair with a tiny window in the wall near the door at the top. I was up the stairs in a minute; I think I took them three at a time. Then, at the door, I stopped. Should I knock? Was this a home? Whose? Would Jan herself answer the door? What would I say? If I left the wooing tulip in my hat, then I would have to wear my hat indoors in order for it to be noticed, and I couldn't do that. Well. I cocked my hat at a rakish angle, and knocked. There was no answer. Was I disturbing someone? Were they reluctant to answer the door? Was she fixing her hair? Or doing something personal? Should I go away? I knocked again, this time making sure to listen hard for any sound of life. There was none.

I pushed the door open. I was in a long hall with a fireplace, a heating stove, a great refectory table at my end, and several brass chandeliers hanging from the rafters down the length of the room. They were unpolished but there were candles in them. Farther down I could see the heads or feet of several beds, some separated from the others by Chinese screens. The windows were old-fashioned and small, set low along the walls. A tall young man appeared from behind one of the screens then, and strode toward me with the air of someone who has just wakened, just washed. I said, "Katje sent me. Is Jan here?" He was strong and fair and I hoped he was not Jan's friend. I hoped she was lonely. Struggling into his cloak, he smiled at me. Like Matt, he answered with a jerk of the head, indicating a door at the far end of the hall. "Probably inside, painting. I just got up." He smiled again, and went on downstairs. I walked down the room to another door.

A girl who paints. I was thinking how wonderful Katje was to have suggested this. Assuming I had another lengthy room ahead, I pushed the door open. But the space was only a fraction of the one I had just crossed. Seekt was obviously a serious patron of the girl's, for on one whole side of the roof he had installed panes of glass. The light was brilliant, the walls a rich cedar. A large easel with rags hanging from it and a new canvas stood in the center of the room. Jan was nowhere to be seen. I began to be afraid that she was a prodigy of some sort, difficult to get along with. Yet probably also lonely; perhaps that's why I was sent. There was a movement in the corner to my left, and someone stood up, back to me. Dark curls falling into place. Oh, but taller than I. Unaware of my presence. Such beautiful curls. The neck stiffened; beautiful muscles, the flesh bulging with life, the shoulders wide, the muscles of the arms, biceps where the cotton blouse clung tight. And the trim waist. "Jan?" I said. Dark curls tumbled upon the forehead as the face of a classical gymnast turned to me; surprised into grandeur, full lips, exquisite, extended lines of the eyebrows. Eyes sharp with surprise, yet soft. Violet eyes, very gentle above such strong cheekbones. "Yes?" he said. I still had my hat on.

I don't want to dwell in that brilliant room in those minutes again. He came toward me out of the shadow, to where light from the skylight illuminated the dark curls. I said, "Katje told me to come and meet you." He reached for my hat, removing it easily, and drew the tulip along the curve of his cheek before placing my hat and then my cloak on a little chair beside the door. It was when he ran the wooing flower along his face that I knew a privileged world of some delicacy, and remoteness, was opening before me. And beauty. An intuition of pleasures beyond the ordinary. I suppose it appealed to my fondness for excitement. Jan introduced himself.

"Did Katje say what should follow our meeting?" he asked.

"No."

He handed me a glass of wine, white wine; pulled a chair beside the easel for me to sit in. He sat opposite me, where light fell directly from the glass roof. In his strongly proportioned face his eyes did not settle down. I sipped the wine.

"Perhaps I should draw you," he said quickly.

"All right."

"Will you let me do a study?" I gulped the wine, nodded. "You can undress there," he said, pointing to a screen behind him. I pretended to be calm, but I think I was entirely in a haze. My heartbeat was a pulsation before my eyes. It was quite unknowingly that I left my cotton underclothes on. I came back out to him and stood, arms at my sides, waiting. He was holding his notebook, but his eyes did not leave mine. We were silent like that for a time. He moved me into the light. He molded my position, his left hand on the side of my head and his right upon my shoulder, then passing along my biceps, moving down my arm, shifting my weight for me. "How do you support yourself?" he asked, but he was not speaking to me. Then his eyes were into mine, and I heard the question again, in ten different voices, and blushed. His hand on my head then, he stroked my hair. I dropped my eyes, but in an instant his other hand was under my chin, lifting my gaze. I thought if he held my eyes to his much longer I would cry. His hand went from my chin; my face dropped just the slightest bit. He pulled me to him, and we were kissing. For a long time. I had never kissed anyone by arrangement before.

When I found my hands inside his shirt I realized that I was quickly, quickly feeling each line and rise and curve, over and over again. I couldn't believe it, and I was terribly happy. I was so proud. I discovered other new things I was newly hungry for. Soon we were both naked on the pallet in that room, and I was possessing with my hands and mouth and legs the perfection of what I myself was, teasing every part of his body with my tongue. Now and then he would stop me, hold me down, and kiss me again. As he fucked me I owned the world and its promise, the moon and the sun; I rode two horses; I handed the man the apple, and took it from her and fucked her; I drank the sea and plowed the earth into furrows of clouds. I looked God in the face and cried, "It's You, it's You!"

As I was dressing, I did not glance over my shoulder at him much, not to seem too eager, though he was standing naked in the sun, waiting. Dressed, I turned and raised my eyes to him. He was holding my hat for me.

"Will you come back?"

"Yes."

"When?"

"Tonight?"

"All right."

He smiled, looking up through the skylight so that the

MY BROTHER'S IMAGE

sun burned in his hair and on his neck. I remember him that way: my hat at his side, a tulip against the big thigh, his neck arched, smiling an ironic smile in the sunlight. Then he looked at me, and somehow the smile entered me, his face becoming serious as his smile seated itself upon my heart, where it faded unaccountably into a little sorrow.

"What time will you come?" he asked.

"Eight. No, there is a dinner. Ten-thirty."

We did not say more. He placed my hat firmly on my head. He led me to the door; opened it. I was going to turn and kiss him, when he slapped my ass, sending me forward into the long room. He was smiling good-bye, both arms up to hold himself in the doorframe where he leaned out toward me, one foot crossed over the other. I gazed back at him, but he motioned me out with a nod.

My day, my home, and my family were not someone else's world any more; they were my world that day. I had a secret.

As I sat through my mother's dinner for Mayor Vilbris's birthday, watching that forceful gentleman dole out his humor across our family's golden table service, I waited only for ten-thirty. I could not stop smiling, knowing that no one could tell the reason for my smile. Moenen sat across the table from me, looking at me in the oddest way. Rolling a golden spoon over and over on the tablecloth, my brother stared at me in the same way I have seen him study a portrait. In the flicker of the candles I thought he was being coy, until I saw that he was not. Unable to guess what he was thinking, I simply let my full joy burst into my eyes, and that disarmed him. He went back to playing the young squire with Vilbris, rolling his golden spoon all the while. When we scraped back our chairs at last, I ran from that dining room. As I rode to Seekt's, the roads lay just for me, under bare trees all planted to await the perfection of that moment. The moon was my confidant. Creation was finished.

I did not know what to say to Matt, so I said nothing. He took my horse. I climbed the circular stairs two at a time, but very slowly. I breathed deeply, pausing at each rise, filling my chest, partly to calm my pulse, partly to absorb each last moment of anticipation, to consume every morsel of this progress into my own place and pleasure in the world.

The door was open. Jan waited for me, leaning on the mantel above the fireplace, firelight hinting along the contours where his shirt and pants followed the forms of his body. He watched me approach, his head cocked to one side. I came within the direct look of his misty eyes, and there was nothing but those eyes, I moving to him. We kissed. After a long time he pulled my head back gently with both hands, looked at me; questioning looks at my cheeks, my lips. My mouth was open, reaching for his as he looked at me. "You look like a hungry baby bird," he laughed. I had his clothes off in no time, and we fell to the floor before the fire.

Then we were lying on his large bed, the firelight dying in its place down the room, its reflections dancing among the dull chandeliers. I told him about myself, about Katje, and the idiot boy. I lay, telling him, inspecting his chest with my lips. He lay, silent, stroking my hair, my butt, listening. He didn't say anything about my story, only stroking me, making encouraging noises. And then he told me about himself. This story, from that night and from other times when he spoke of himself, I tell you now:

Jan was born in a cobbler's family in the little country town of Soest, outside Amsterdam. Jan had six brothers and a sister, Lise. As young children, he and Lise played in the fields and around the market stalls together. He was devoted to Lise, and sometimes in the afternoons he would sit combing her hair, which was long. One night when Jan was twelve and Lise eleven, the cobbler broke his wife's head open with a mug of gin. Although the field they lived in wasn't theirs, they buried their mother in it. The cobbler was taken away for the navy.

Jan's brothers ran away to the woods where there lived a gang of children who begged and robbed. Jan took Lise to the only hiding place he knew, which was their parson's woodshed. They were permitted to stay there, and they lived on scraps from the parson's table. Lise found work keeping house for the town seamstress. After a few months she told Jan that the seamstress was taking her to Amsterdam, where she would be cared for by the great ladies. She did not cry, but Jan cried; they hugged each other and parted.

Soon Jan was doing chores around the parsonage, although the parson's wife did not like him. The parson was a shy man. Despite that, he visited the poor and the sick in his parish a great deal. On Sundays he preached with a low voice, as though calming an unruly mob. As he reasoned things out before his congregation, you could tell that he had known harsh times.

They celebrated Jan's birthdays. When Jan was fourteen the parson's wife made a large meal. She had grown tolerant of Jan, although she openly and quite unreasonably made trouble whenever he spent any time alone with her husband. As they finished their food, the parson reached out and put his hand over Jan's hand on the table. The wife looked hard at her husband and made a noise like a dog coughing. There was only silence from him. In the silence, Jan turned his bold violet eyes on the parson.

"Jan, I have decided that you must now go to the city, into a situation that will afford you more advantages than there are here. I have been in touch with Herr van Seekt, a friend from my university days. He has agreed to take you in his charge, and to teach you, moreover, the bookseller's trade. I have told him about your industry, your strength, and your good manners. He is returning from Germany, and tomorrow he will arrive here on his way home. You should be ready to leave with him."

Jan's eyes danced.

"One thing further. You are a fine, and in some ways an extraordinary, lad. Your task in life is a special one. Christ told us that a most important inner mood is charity. Charity. Remember the word. If, Jan, you ponder on that word, you may prosper. Do you remember our talks about charity? Bear in mind always that Jan's golden key lies somewhere among the many applications of that word. If you give the gift of your conclusions about charity in word or deed to the situation in which you find yourself at any moment, you will prevail. That is your strength now—charity."

Jan and the parson continued to look at each other for a long moment.

"To aid your diligence in life, I give you my gold watch, so that you never need to look upon the world as a poor man."

"Oh, sir." Jan hugged the parson quite hard, and then bolted from the kitchen. He ran down the lane to his older friend, Willem, whom he found sitting under the willow tree on the canal. Willem was eighteen and was drinking beer in the dusk. Jan told Willem he was leaving Soest, and Willem said he would keep Jan's mug for him. He asked where Jan was going. For some reason, Jan didn't know why, Jan said he was going to his uncle's farm in the north. Willem laughed. There were only cows in the north, he said. Then Willem did what he had been doing to Jan recently, he took him in his arms. Stroking Jan's hair, he called Jan names. Jan blushed. He lifted himself on his toes and kissed Willem on the cheek, and ran away fast through the clover field. In the light from the shimmering water, Willem stood, kicking the root of the willow tree. Once he looked up and waved toward the night where Jan had disappeared.

It was a big carriage, with two men in the box and a horse tied behind. Four lathered horses sprayed and stomped in the yard, and after a long time the three watching people saw the carriage door thrust open. Tassels swung along the top of the little window in the door as it fell open toward the ground. Jan had seen the black and gold tassels swinging even before the carriage stopped. It had not occurred to Jan to be frightened about Herr Seekt, and now he was fascinated with the carriage. Seekt bulged out the doorframe and bumped to the earth, hove himself off the carriage side with his left arm, and took a stance with his hand at his neck. He greeted his friend the parson and then, eyeing them all as if from a distant height, he said, "Mary!" His eyes danced, and he fanned his wrist with all its heavy lace, fanning his neck and his unbewigged head. Everybody smiled except the coachman, who looked as if he were watching this from somewhere down the road. The parson's wife smiled at the horses. Jan smiled. Seekt beamed. The distant coachman's whip had an ornamented handle. It looked to be made of ebony. The parson's wife watched the length of the whip sinking into the mud where the horses stomped. Jan said, "Herr Seekt, my guardian has told me the good news, and I am ready to go with you. Would you stop with us here, before . . ." and Jan put aside his head to think.

Seekt said, "Yes, I certainly will, Jan, thank you. You know, I bought this coach from a countess in Dresden, a real countess, Jan, and my man Matt there thinks it's the silliest conveyance since the French carried armor." The distant coachman's expression did not change when he heard his name. The wife's eyes, stunned with country living, followed a big black fly among the horses' hooves. Seekt said, "Come, my lady," and she felt quite gay walking into her house on his big arm.

The leaves of chestnut trees were thick with late evening, passing by the windows. The dim light of Seekt's reading candle lit the black and gold silk trimmings of the bulky coach. Seekt was constantly busy, shuffling foolscap, reading, adjusting his angle of vision in the candlelight. Jan sometimes hung his head from the window and his hair planed behind him in the wind. Seekt pulled Jan in by his frock. Then he squirmed through the window of the rollicking coach and shouted through the night to the coachman, "Matt! Stop and see the boys on the way, Matt." Seekt prodded his way back through the window to his seat, and they talked about what books the parson had given Jan. Jan busied himself putting some of Herr Seekt's papers into boxes. He spent some of his time studying the ornate lettering, and Seekt did not interrupt him to say how the papers should be arranged.

The coach pulled off the road at a little old church. Bounced to a halt, jolting. The coachman jumped down. Insects cascaded immediately through the windows, batting against their heads. "Knew we were coming," said Seekt as he and Jan made for opposite doors. The candle went out by itself.

Matt had taken a posture against a bank of foliage, in the dark, distinguished by the pissing sound. Jan and

Seekt made a pair at the hedge nearer the coach. Insects had followed them, and Seekt swatted at his head with his arm of lace. "Get away!" A soft, insistent music came from the church, though it appeared to be abandoned. "They're home!" said Seekt, moving toward the small pointed arch where the darkness thickened. "Former wards of mine," he said, bustling on ahead. From indoors, starlight imitated dawn beyond the chapel's six small windows, and the altar was lit by two giant white candles. "I bought this for the boys when they moved out," Seekt whispered to Jan as they stood in the dark entry. Two young men were sitting on high stools facing each other by the candles, playing Spanish guitars. They played a contrapuntal melody with the wide intervals of Gregorian chant in it, very fast. They played staring straight at each other's faces, eyes fixed on each other's eyes. Jan and Seekt listened in the dark, departing soon without interrupting. In the coach, they hugged each other before embarking down the short road to the city. The single horse, a roan, galloped behind. When the coach slowed, she shook her head on the braces, ringing the leather and metal tackle. She pranced, neighing at the expiring stars in the morning sky above the city gate. Jan and Seekt slept, lying on their seats.

Jan lived in the quarters for apprentices. Forming a wing of Seekt's house, the rooms stretched along the back garden above the stables. There were no other apprentices, and Jan had the long gallery to himself, with beds, bookshelves, a great porcelain stove, old musical instruments, and easels. Seekt also had a large dining table for the boys with great chandeliers hanging above it, quite brilliant though in some disrepair. Jan employed himself in dusting the books of Seekt's library, or running errands, and on his own time he played among the tools of culture in the long gallery. One night, soon after arriving, he cajoled Maria, the cook, batting about her huge skirts as she worked, teasing her with pleasantries, to allow him to watch Seekt eat dinner with a Spanish general. Jan peeked through the door at the candlelight on polished mahogany and silver. Often, then, if he ate dinner alone in quarters, Jan lighted a few of the candles remaining in the chandeliers and drank a little wine. Sometimes he and Seekt read together in Seekt's study. Seekt made an effort to give Jan the substance of the stories of Homer, and they read a dialogue by Plato, which Seekt had translated.

On his errands, Jan saw the city, and in his first summer there began taking long walks alone. Soon, too, he was introduced to the two guitar players when they came to visit Seekt. Frederick was their names, both of them. They were nineteen and twenty. Though they no longer worked for Seekt, Frederick One and Two saw him frequently. When he was tired or in a fitful humor it often struck Seekt to visit One and Two, staying in the parsonage of their little see on his land in the country. Usually Jan accompanied him. They taught Jan how to ride. They were handsome, in an open-shirted sort of way. On visits to the country, Jan helped the Fredericks to repair the chapel roof, which was their continuing project. The summer came and went, and the three of them, Jan almost as tall as the older two, tore through the fields or worked on the roof or made big dinners for an approving Seekt. The Fredericks cooked; Jan served them all, and washed. On these holidays Seekt became at times fairly dotty with pleasure and praised the weather incessantly, fanning himself and saying, "Mary, isn't it nice!" He behaved in a silly way, and talked occasionally about his wife, who had been very lively, or about Katje at Versailles.

In town that winter, the Fredericks took Jan skating. They taught him to paint with oils, and slept in quarters when they stayed. Jan often heard them come in late at night, a little tipsy, and fall into their beds at the far end of the gallery. Once he got up to talk to them, and as he carried his candle down the gallery its light caught them in an embrace, clad only in their drooping socks. They were holding each other around the neck and kissing. Their muscles rippled and relaxed as they turned to face Jan; the light shone on their skin. "Fifteen is too young for girls to kiss," they said, for it had been Jan's fifteenth birthday the day before. Jan laughed with them, and then he salivated quite forcefully for a few seconds and put out his candle with a big shot of spit. As he lay down in his bed he heard the two of them move along the gallery saying

"Shhh" very loudly to each other. Jan slipped off his covers, but he had an erection, so he turned onto his stomach, arching his ass a little. For added insufferableness, he pretended to snore. "What a pretty virgin," Frederick One whispered, as four hands reached for Jan's shoulders and turned him over, holding him down. Jan saw the outlines of pectorals and triceps and biceps as they held him in the moonlight. Frederick One's dark hair fell on Jan's neck as One whispered, "It will be better for you if you do not try to resist." They giggled, holding Jan, who had thrust toward their faces making loud, ludicrous kissing noises. "Look, you," said Two, coming nose to nose with Jan, his sternness so obviously a pretense that everyone became a trifle shy. Jan's left arm shot free and curled around Two's neck in such an eager hold that all they could do after that was kiss. As Jan lifted his back he felt a woolly, socked foot slip under his ass.

"There are still some painters in Amsterdam," said Seekt. He was standing in quarters, where Jan had invited him for tea, looking at a table covered by Jan's charcoal sketches. "So if it's an artist you want to be, I think we can give you a fine start, Jan. Why don't you take these over to Doorn's studio tomorrow?" Jan was chinning himself on one of the roof beams, but he nodded at Seekt as energetically as he could. "I'll give you a letter for Doorn before you go. I don't think I've tasted this tea before, have I?"

"Ouch." Jan thundered to the floor, landing on all fours. He stood up. "I bought it at the India store. The boy said the emperor of India drinks it every morning, but I don't believe that. Is it good, Herr Seekt? Would you like to drink it every morning?"

"You are built like an Italian statue, Jan. You can go and show off in the anatomy classes at the medical academy. You go and pose for them, and they won't have to cut anybody up. How do you make tea here? Does that hearth still work?"

Jan showed him the domestic arrangements, and how he had been cooking his own meals in quarters for some time, having borrowed several essential kitchen implements from Maria. Some evenings Matt poked his head in to ask how Jan was getting along. One night when Matt was returning from a late errand, Jan brought him upstairs and warmed him some dinner. Matt didn't talk much, but after the meal he went out and got a belt in tooled leather that he had been making. A large belt, wide. Though it fitted Jan well, Jan didn't suppose it might have been made for him.

Jan carried Seekt's note to Doorn, and some months later he carried back a note from Doorn to Seekt. After reading it, Seekt gave it to Jan.

Patroon:
Greetings. Jan progresses well in studies of perspective, anatomy, and drawing from life. We hope to show you some work of diverse kinds soon. He has talent. He alarms me a little. My respects to you.

"Good work," said Frederick One, dismounting and handing the note to Two. "Does Doorn touch you? He used to have quite a reputation, you know."

"He never tried anything," said Jan, dropping a swift curtsy.

"Good girl," said Frederick Two. "Doorn used to be seen regularly down on the plage."

"What's the plage?" asked Jan, omitting to curtsy.

"The sailors' wharf," said One, unbuckling his saddle. "You know, where we meet our navy."

"Oh, yes," said Jan. "They've started wearing different colored scarves around their necks. It's a code that tells what you like to do in bed. Blue is supposed to mean they like to play the girl."

"What's your favorite color, soldier?" asked Two as they folded Jan's arms behind his back.

"In truth," One said, releasing Jan, "you had better be careful about being in such places. Mayor Vilbris has been singing a song recently about sweeping the streets around the harbor. Our friend the burgess told us that our mayor has become quite devout since his wife died, and that he is particularly splenetic when the clergy of the city complain to him about what they call unnatural acts."

"What are unnatural acts?" asked Jan, grabbing both Fredericks by the ass simultaneously.

The rooster came at Jan's neck again and again, kissing. The feathers and ribbons in the rooster's headdress tickled Jan where his chest was bare, and he began giggling and shouting, "Stop it. Stop it!" The rest of the rooster was plainly a slim girl in a red silk gown. As she crashed into the dark bushes and vanished under a Chinese lantern, Jan got his last glimpse of her; her bare foot shining for an instant above the grass. Bare feet seemed an admirable piece of daring. Jan's costume was a cobbler's loose leather pantaloons, a white silk frock open to the waist, the belt Matt had given him, and a simple black mask for his face.

At eighteen, Jan had made for himself a career as a portrait painter. But not quite enough of a career that he would have expected to be invited to a costume ball given by the new governor of our East India Company. Governor Iselin's house on the canal was famous for its gardens, its hedges cut in fantastic shapes, and its fancifully curved and ornamented brick wall. When the invitation arrived at the little room Seekt had made for Jan's studio, Jan whistled. Immediately he pictured himself wearing something quite unlike the opulent dress recently being copied from France. So it was Jan the Cobbler who stood at the bottom of the garden, where Iselin's brick wall, high as your head, curved from the water in a perfect round toward him. He entered its gate between brick pillars capped with twin sandstone astrolabes. Beneath the astrolabes, Jan stared at a sandstone-block stairway that descended along the inner arc of the brick wall rounding the boat slip. Jan paced down to the beribboned barges that knocked against the white stone blocks of Iselin's slip. He stood in the light from a Chinese lantern hanging high in the trees above the garden wall. Looking up, he saw the rooster's head disappear and a tree branch tremblingly resume its place. From her arms, Jan had judged that the rooster was probably quite too young for parties. He resolved to make a gesture for the girl later, one so gallant as to give her something to remember besides having followed him around that night.

MY BROTHER'S IMAGE

In a square maze of chest-high box bush allèes up in the garden, Jan saw a beautiful woman skimming along the hedge in the company of a giant dodo bird. When he saw them down the length of the next allèe, Jan turned and stopped. The dodo was wearing an iridescent white waistcoat beneath the enormous and realistically feathered head. The lady was superb, blond hair piled in four neat, graceful rolls. She was Diana, for she carried a bow. Slender arms. The lady's forehead swept from the peak of her coif to the tip of her nose. In the moonlight, her figure was luminous. The gravel, almost as small as sand, whispered and hinted as the couple progressed toward Jan. When she passed into the glow of the lantern, he saw that the lady held a sleeping rabbit in the crook of her left arm and, further, that the lady was his sister. Jan and Lise laughed and hugged each other. The dodo vanished in the dark. The bunny woke up. Jan held Lise's left arm where the bunny was and flashed his grin into her eyes. They forgave each other for everything. A wry grin, you might say. She reached out with her right hand, dropping her hunting gear, and tugged on his belt, saying, "Jan. Jan."

Lise told him she had lived in Versailles as a lady-in-waiting to the Dutch ambassador's wife. King Louis of France enjoyed watching her and she was frequently permitted to see the king eat. She said she sometimes also helped the king's mistress to bathe. They told each other all that was necessary. She told him about the recent autopsy of the Austrian princess, attended by three hundred knights and ladies of France, with ambassadors from Austria. For important foreign princes, it was proof of the absence of foul play, it was a social occasion, everything. In the last century, they'd opened the beloved Anne of England, monsieur's wife, and the smell was so awful that no one could stay. Lise said she didn't look at the princess's body.

When the brother and sister said good-night they agreed to write letters to each other. Jan watched her misted shape, holding arrows and bow and the rabbit, growing intermittent in the dark. In an instant, Jan was being pelted by a gaggle of merchants' wives with questions and eyebrows and commissions. Under the Chinese lantern, they came like moths. He walked with them until they buzzed away by a tall hedge clipped into pyramids and diamonds. There was no lantern near Jan but the moon was strong. He was alone in the moonlight. The people were tiresome and his sister had gone. The rooster came toward him, suddenly illuminated against the diamonds and pyramids. As she passed, he could see the rooster head hesitating to look his way. He moved beside her, saying, "You look very beautiful." Jan bowed and the frightened rooster curtsied, and then she immediately ran away into the trees. Then a boy costumed in a small mask appeared. His attire was unusually rich, but not at all fanciful. The boy stopped by Jan. He said, "Did you accost that girl?"

"No," said Jan.

"We won't have any of that. I've seen you. You paint, don't you?"

No reply.

"Come, would you like to paint my portrait? I am of one of the great families. Will you paint me, sir?"

"Not here," said Jan. "What is your name?"

"This is a *masked* ball," said the stranger. A cardinal of the Spanish church passed, in robes of their particular red. Passing, moonlight on his silver-white hair, he put his arm upon the young stranger's shoulder, saying, "Moenen, Moenen," and drawing the boy along. "Fighting again?" Jan heard the prelate say before they were gone into the dark. Jan went to find his boat then, he remembers. He rowed himself home that night.

That autumn, and winter, Jan got to know Katje. She visited him with Lise. They got along. Before Katje and Lise went back to court, Katje told Jan about me.

"So you have met my twin?" I asked, lying in the dark on our first night.

It was almost dawn. I made him make love to me again, and he slept immediately after. That early, purple-gray light drifted to the windowsill by the head of our bed. Suddenly our candle was a ghost. It was still, airlessly so.

When Jan shifted the position of his leg, the cotton sheet whispered. Even that low noise seemed to dwell in the room's corners. I lay with my head on his shoulder, tasting his skin with my tongue every now and again. One single bird, somewhere outside in the winter morning, stabbed its song into the frosted light.

CHAPTER THREE

IT IS NICE to have someone. Someone who has chosen you, someone who is pleasing, can double your force in life and make the rough places smooth. It is as if creation says to you, "Yes, we've been waiting for you, and we have just the thing. See?" One feels answered. Who can deny it? And, then, there is that special alchemy of the agreement when both people admit they feel quite strongly for each other. Nothing like it. Everyone should know it. Once, or more? Once, with a lifetime of elaborating on the agreement? Some old married couples seem bored. Perhaps they have gone beyond the personal in the romantic sense, and romance is boring to them. In almost everyone else I observe, lingering about their eyes, the ghost of an agreement to excite and esteem. A ghost of paradise in the eyes of those who have felt as strongly as this, and shared it with someone for a time.

Still, in this loving business, this proud surrendering, I think there is often some element of regret or risk. I think some of the sweetness comes from how superhuman it is to glory and pleasure oneself in one's ideals. How far from humble to touch the image of one's desire, call it one's own, to be pressed into a coy embrace by life itself, and then insist on that embrace. To be able to say to life, "Be all I have dreamed," makes the conceit turn real for a time. We can command the world like gods. But the risk, the impossibility, are part of the deliciousness.

At sixteen, I felt the feelings, but did not know them. The first of our mornings together, I woke in Jan's bed to open the music box of the day. The hour or two we would spend dressing and eating were private. Simple acts were intriguing things. Knowing the fractious, blushing wonders of my own body, to know also the power and delight of making his body respond to me—magical too. I was probably all over him; I remember I would sit between his legs, right underneath him, while he shaved.

"How can I concentrate?" he would ask.

"On what?"

"Now, stop it. If you're going to sit there, behave. Who will trust my portraiture if I arrive all cut up? Put some water over the fire. Go. Go."

And at last I would go make tea, after he had, carefully balancing, slid his foot and ankle along the crack of my ass, caressing tightly there. This is a good way to make a boy do your will—to hold him firmly, yet gently, underneath like that.

At his door then, above the winding stair, I would dart up and catch him around the neck and kiss his ear.

"Nooo . . ." he would say.

Home then, those winter mornings, back among the little people. I mean that, from my new remove to heaven, the family and their concerns seemed precious and inconsequential. I stopped in my mother's room occasionally, at the time when she was having her breakfast. Acres of white lace, her bed and bonnet, in the icy silver light from the windows. She was then, for me, a person, rather than my mother. For the first time I had a critical angle on her, enough dispassion to sense her as a wholly separate being. I could be amused, rather than galled and faintly threatened by her foibles, her enthusiasms. One morning, as she had her coffee and iced radishes, a frequent breakfast in bed, I got an idea which proved felicitous. I asked for the use of a suite of rooms above the long gallery, a suite that had a private staircase and a door onto our courtyard. I gave no reason, just said I wanted to move into those rooms for a time. I think the reason mother allowed this was that she made me realize immediately the increased cost of heating them if I were to live there. That became an opportunity for me to meet costs out of my own inheritance, a good exercise in money responsibility. After we'd made strict promises about the money, I was allowed to use those rooms. Only at the end of our conversation did I catch a worldly look in my mother's eyes. She asked me, idly, what I was going to do in the rooms. As I was explaining that I wanted to see what it would be like to live on my own, or some such thing, I noticed Mother watching me with quite a bit of warmth and fondness, a little pride in her eyes. Then a tiny wisp, almost a sea breeze, of sorrow lifted her eyebrows, and I went to her and we hugged. She crunched a radish very sharply as I left her room.

That was exciting, getting my own quarters ready to surprise Jan. I chose two rooms at the end of the gallery that had big windows and a fine view of the canal, windmills far in the frosty distance. There was a beautifully paneled little door in the last of the rooms, our bedroom. The staircase wound right down beside the glass dome where I'd met the swami that night. I liked to think of that. I began using the private door immediately; and on one of the first occasions, as I unlocked it, I paused there to draw a heart in the frost on one of the large glass panes, with Jan's and my initials in it. Indiscreet, but I never thought that way then. I had some furniture moved in, trying to keep it as spare as possible. I became cross with myself when I realized that I was trying hard to have things that would impress Jan. Then, one day, when a particularly fine set of wall fixtures disappeared from the main hall, I had a run-in with Moenen about it. I was approaching my own door, feet squeaking in the packed snow, when my twin appeared around the corner.

"Steen," he said.

I looked at him, my eyes tearing profusely in the wind off the canal, and suddenly I moved to cut off his view of the frosted initials I had drawn. His cloak whipped behind him with that popping sound a flag sometimes makes.

"Steen," he purred, "do you know those two Venetian mirrors that used to be in the foyer of the library, the ones with the candle mounts and the silver almost gone from the backs?" I nodded. "Father used to say you could see the ghosts of Venice dance there when their candles were lighted again. Remember Mother telling us that?"

I nodded.

"What happened to them?"

"Moenen, I haven't seen you since Mother and I arranged it, but I am moving into these rooms over the gallery."

"Mother said something to me, yes," said Moenen. "And so you wanted those mirrors for yourself?"

"Yes, in fact," I said.

"Along with the silver wall fixtures from the hall? Well, fine. If you want my underwear for anything, or my signet ring to melt down for a toothpick, just ask. Or, as you have done thus far, don't ask. I tried to visit your palace, but you've locked the doors that connect from the house, so I'm reduced to begging at your tower door here in the cold. What are you doing up there, Steen?"

"Come up and see what I've done already, Brother," I said. I noticed that as I unlocked the door I kept the key well hidden from his view, though I knew he could never copy it just from sight.

He was my first guest in my rooms. As I opened the door at the top Moenen made that dry cough in his throat which has since become his signal that he is trying to be very impartial, a Christian gentleman. Entering, I showed him the great platform bed with rich tapestry hangings that I had installed.

Moenen quickly removed his broad hat, as he does on entering any distinguished house, and laid it with his cloak upon a chair. Then he went around the rooms, nodding his assent at the harmony of the appointments. He ended, hands folded behind his back, rocking on his heels before one of the large windows. Gazing on the canal and the countryside beyond, not glancing at me even once, he said, "Very nice." Rocking slightly on his heels.

I was full of joy because of my new adventure. I wanted to share with him, to bring him alive. I went to him and put my hands on his shoulders to stop his rocking. "What are you doing these days? Are you excited about anything?" I asked. He tossed his head with a brief laugh and disengaged his shoulders. Seating himself near the window, he said that he was attending meetings of the mayor's special council.

"Are you actually a member?" I asked. "Aren't you too young?"

"I suppose not. The cardinal had me named a permanent adviser, so I attend every meeting. It seems they want our family represented."

"What for? What are the meetings about?"

"Well," intoned Moenen, "it seems things have reached a pretty shocking pass here in Amsterdam. We're becoming a sort of degenerate Italian backwater by the looks of it, not a solid northern capital like we used to be. Vices are being practiced openly now that decent people would have blushed even to hear about a few years ago. We are worried about the effect on the young, on future generations. If rites of pleasure for its own sake, if unnatural extremes, are not checked, who knows where it may lead? What families, what traditions, may it not corrupt?"

"Will you have tea, Moenen?" I asked after a moment. "I can prepare food here too, you know. Or brandy or beer?"

"Tea, I suppose," he said.

As I prepared his tea, I asked, "Would you strike at public drunkenness, or gambling among workers?"

"Well, there's a good deal of money in both those things, Steen. You and I both know that it wouldn't do to offend certain interests if we can avoid it. No, our idea is to hit directly at licentiousness, prostitution, perversion and the like—we want to strengthen the moral fiber of our populace. Trade is down. None of the young men will work the ships any more—too busy, too tired from taking their pleasure all the time."

"Moenen, that's absurd. The navy's always been that way, always will be. And every ship available is fully manned. It's just that there aren't enough ships, not since the Regent de Witt decided to buy English naval protection rather than maintain a fighting navy of our own. What you're talking about has nothing to do with our navy. Who could start such a stupid crusade? Who is behind this? Whose idea was this? Tell me."

Moenen would not look at me then. He tried to shake the whole conversation off like a dog shaking off water. He took his teacup from me and held it resolutely, gazing through the window. "I don't know who started it," he barked, "that's what they were discussing at the time I was invited to attend, and they've been on the subject ever since. It is very complicated, Steen, because they are very serious about it. They plan to make arrests and prosecutions in a systematic way from now on. So they need all the power of the city and all our influence with the regent, in order that this can be legal and thorough. I think it

MY BROTHER'S IMAGE

started in the churches, though why the mayor takes their cause so hard, I don't know. It's strange because the cardinal says nothing to me about this outside the meetings, not ever."

"What's the usual conversational topic with him, Brother?" I asked. "Inquisitions to remember? Ten favorite penances?"

"Steen. Do you mind? I'm really sorry, but someone has to keep this family on top, represent us. Do you mind, Steen, if I just try to keep you in silks for another generation or so? Do you mind?"

I patted his shoulder, but he shook me off. He leaned against the windowsill. He said, "I'm only sixteen."

That made me think how rarely he was human any more; it made me sad. I pulled a chair near to him and crossed my legs. All we could hear was the ticking of the clock. We both sat there in the silence.

"Moenen," I said, "do you remember three summers ago when the regent visited us on the farm? It was only two days, wasn't it? He needed somewhere to spend the night. Do you remember the excitement?" He nodded. "Remember how flustered we all were, since the herald had only given us a few hours' notice? Having to remember all we knew about entertaining princes, and to prepare all the empty bedrooms, order the slaughter, and set the cooks to work. We sent riders to fetch the neighborhood girls; I remember you wanted to do that, but mother said you had to supervise the slaughter instead. She gave you a list—so many sheep and ducks and so forth. Did you have the overseers actually do the killing?"

"Yes, Peter and his lame son did it, mostly," Moenen said.

"And the carriages arrived at dusk, remember? And we were ready for them after all, weren't we?"

"No, that's typical. We weren't ready for them, though you and mother seemed ready to sit down and make merry." Moenen's dry cough salted the air again.

"I didn't want to make merry, Moenen. I hated it. I ran away."

"Well, you see, *I* was still in the kitchens, of course," my brother said to the window, "because a hogshead of beer was wedged in the wine-cellar steps; nothing could move up or down; no one knew what to do. I went and shouted for more men; I pulled some lout away from his spit at the fire and I made them work at it, but the harder they tried, the worse they fared. I heard revelry in the dining rooms and I screamed at them 'Get the ax!' We smashed that cask in no time, split it wide open, and the wood and beer crashed down the stairs—a river of beer. They all got wet, and started to laugh. As I ordered them down for the wines, I heard mother's voice from the top of the steps. She took me into a corner of the kitchen. Firelight reddened her face. I heard the lamb stewing and popping on its spit as she reprimanded me. She demanded to know why I could never leave things alone and enjoy myself! It was the first time, Steen, that I realized our mother didn't perhaps like me all that much. She left me, and I straightened my suit. When I went in, I found that there were no places at the host's table, with mother and the regent. I looked at mother, and finally she called me and introduced me very briefly to the regent, then sent me away. You know what I did? I took a bottle of wine to the stables and I got drunk and went to sleep. Lovely. I didn't see you in the dining room. Where did you spend the evening, Steen?"

"Moenen, I thought you'd hate it. I stole us some food and I went to the millpond to wait for you. Remember, I said I would. Didn't you remember?"

He looked at me hard, then very suddenly he turned his head away, got his hat and cloak, and went for the door. With his hand on the knob he paused, and I heard him draw a breath rather noisily. Silent, he raised his arm toward me as if to make a point while speaking. His arm hesitated . . . and fell. Then he was gone.

Soon after that, one cold night, a winter midnight, Jan came to visit in my new rooms for the first time. I had the fire blazing. When he held me, everything else became small-sized, manageable and forgivable.

"I should make a picture of you, here in your own home. This is your first time on your own, isn't it? How does it feel to be a man?" he asked.

Then I told him about Moenen, what he was doing. Jan became grave. He wouldn't explain; he only held my head, and looked at me very sadly for a time.

I remember my room, that night, or some night soon

after that. Candles. I remember a moment kissing Jan, my hand on the back of his neck. I looked into the mirror in that room, sideways at the profile of the two of us, nearly equally tall, kissing. Romance is an unpredictable quality in the composition of a life, I thought. As singular a quality in a person's inner constellation as is the palm of a hand. In my memory, I break our kiss and move my hand to the little round convex mirror. Working like a singular human hand—I've been to the anatomy classes in Amsterdam—my hand approaches the mirror in a halo of firelight. The mirror catches the lines on my pink palm, like the surface of a red moon coming closer. In memory, Jan regards me as my hand closes with the mirror, palm first, fingers over the wooden frame. I hold the mirror up so both of us can see each other in it. A handsome portrait—our eyes, dark blond hair—but he turns soon to the big bed. I do not know if I actually held a mirror up to us that night, and now I will never know if it happened that night or later. Is memory less creative than this?

That night we talked, lying in bed; I remember what we said. We had made love, the fire was dying in a rich warmth on the hearth near us. I kissed and kissed his stomach, and when he rolled over I darted my tongue over the curves of his buttocks, timing it so it would always be a surprise. *"Ach,"* Jan said, and caught at me to make me stop teasing. I wrestled until he got his hand firmly in the crack of my butt, just behind my balls, cradling me there. I became quiet, holding onto him around the back of his neck and staring at him.

"Poor Moenen," I said.

"Ah," said Jan, patting me, looking at me as I had looked at the idiot boy.

"Jan, I want them to know about us; I want us to be written and sung about. When we're like this, I want to have the country house all to ourselves, with hundreds of servants, to give balls and masques, to entertain all the beautiful young people in all Europe. We could become famous. Do you think I could get the country house all to myself, Jan? I could get lawyers, and—"

"That's not it," he replied, so quietly that I still remember the exact phrase, and the clock ticking. "You're in the wrong place at the wrong time." I looked, waiting for him to explain. When I didn't understand, he always explained. "What happens if the caterpillar tries to flutter its wings and fly?" Jan asked. "What happens if the butterfly, mourning a windless day, tries to crawl among the miniature leaves like a tiny worm, and tears its wings? Our lives are this, prince," he grunted. He reached, his body flexing, down into the hearth, and grabbed a burning stick. "Our lives are this, each moment . . ." He held the twig before my eyes and shook out the small flame at its tip, smartly, so that it glowed no more. "Be of the flame! The joy is here now, but you dream it into the future. What do you fear? It's yours, and you don't need people to witness it for you, prove to you that it's yours. It's yours, that's all. All the solutions may happen now, if you will tell yourself the truth."

"And all the problems; they must be here now too, no?" I snuggled.

"True."

So I slept draped on his chest again, before the fire died. Funny, I remember my dream; of pennants fluttering atop pavilions, a courtly jousting tournament with knights in armor. Jan and I were jousting. Each lowered his visor at opposite ends of the lists; sun struck the armor as we spurred our horses toward each other. As the trumpets fell silent you heard only the thunder of horses, or *saw* only thunder, in the silence of dreams. I realized that one of us was weaponless, with no lance. I ended the dream, reminding myself, as I fell through sleep, that Jan had just warned me against dreaming. Himself asleep by then, he held me. The fire was still glowing.

Near the end of that winter, a traveling deputation came from Versailles. They included Lise, Jan's sister. Monsieur Rameau, the composer and keyboard virtuoso at the French court, was to play in Amsterdam. Some of the great French families came, too. It was a lavish end to our icy social season of the winter months. Katje didn't come. She stayed in France with her viscomte. Lise, traveling with the family of our ambassador to Versailles, got to visit with Jan.

The night of the concert, I ordered our coach to be fitted with sleds, since the great snowfall of the afternoon would make fast running indeed that night. It is one of my pleasures in winter to have a coach warm, cozy, and well provided with spirits and foods. That night we packed hams in thin slices, a mild cheese, some caviar, and several bottles of a very clear white wine. And one bottle of port for the party following the concert. Tonight's after-host, our ambassador and Lise's patron, had the sense to invite everyone to his country house so all the horses and carts could have a run on a white winter night.

The concert hall was a sort of peacock alley. Since the Dutch stopped fighting the French, many of us had begun to imitate them, especially in gaudy dress. Some of the young men who followed Lise to the ambassador's box wore all the silks and laces a tailor could provide. Not a few of them wore makeup, with faces as heavily powdered as their wigs. But again, mind you, those staid, darker figures, the old burghers with their families chatting in the lobby, these men would not impute any vanity, any quality of perspective at all to their prized sons. I know them. The same shortsightedness that has made the Netherlands a rich client of the English navy operates in their homes, and a son's second beauty mark passes without giving them a moment's pause to ponder the richness of human nature. They do not know the innocent yearnings of their favorite eggs to be noticed, admired.

The burghers herded their families into that lobby like fat ganders under the waving plumes of their hats. Their eyes mirrored the same concerns I see there at meetings of our East Indies Corporation—the iris counts one million, two million, while shadows of their strutting, mercantile god play on their arched brows. Their wives have caught that same smug, proud cast of face; I wondered that the children with them did not freeze.

The mayor had the temerity to bring his dog, attired in red and gold. I mean the mayor was in red and gold. The dog was undressed except for a big studded collar. The mayor treated concerts and plays in a very odd way. His wife was dead, and he never attended an actual performance, only the activities before and after. His children didn't attend. Very unconventional. I remember him standing on the lobby stairs; lace, scarlet and gold coat, one step above a group of burghers, head thrown back, arms crossed on his chest, big hunter dog looking up at him and slobbering. I'll say this for him, he did wear his dark hair curled, without a wig. Jan and I went past them below. I saw Moenen leaning against the banister, lost in thought, a cherub.

As we sat, Jan pointed out to me the Spanish cardinal, who was sitting with one of our town's Catholic families. They were the only group in the hall who seemed to be enjoying themselves. As the cardinal laughed I marked his sharp features; a hooked nose, with bright, birdlike eyes, stringy white hair under his crimson cap. As he laughed he was holding the crucifix at his chest in his bony hands. The picture has stayed with me.

We read the program. This was to be a harpsichord competition between the visiting German virtuoso from England, Herr Handel, and the master from the French court, Monsieur Rameau. Each played his own compositions, then after the second intermission they were both to extemporize a set of variations on a theme which would be given them. As the musicians waited before us following the intermission, two young persons marched down the aisle to present them with their theme. One was an odd girl in peasant clothes, blond and with a maddeningly wide bodice exposing a smooth chest which seemed as if it was just beginning to form. The other, a boy, was dressed in pastel silks, with white hose and a little lace. Curly, curly chestnut hair, as if each ringlet had been wound individually. Her hand on his arm, they walked past us, and I saw in his gait a poise he must have learned when being presented at court. His stately manner startled me. As he passed, I saw that his eyes were glazed, bright wet. When they reached the front they bowed to the musicians. Then the boy bent over Herr Handel's harpsichord to state the theme. He faltered, and suddenly careened sideways, bumping into Herr Handel's chair, and began to giggle. There was a murmur. I heard people asking who the children were, and what was wrong with the boy. The shepherdess went to him and whispered and he calmed down. Then she addressed Herr Handel's keyboard and, with a delicate touch, played a slow and rather grave saraband. It was a lovely moment, the girl's one finger picking out a simple melody while we all, musicians included, gaped at the pair of them. The theme done, the girl curtsied to the house, and helped the boy to stand. She walked him firmly, and as gracefully as she could, out a side door.

Handel played first, but our Dutch manners almost drowned him out. I heard people identify the boy as being attached to an important French personage; but though many said they recognized the girl, none could name her. Handel stopped playing his second variation to wait for quiet. He got it. We then sat through two impressive displays, with the prize going to Monsieur Rameau. As he held his flowers and the purse, he looked down at us all in what I thought was a remarkably acerbic manner, as if he were sorry that he had created the Netherlands after all. Lise, afterward, said she must ride in the ambassador's carriage. As we parted she told me she, too, had seen the girl somewhere. She knew the boy at Versailles, and she promised to tell me about him later.

Imagine, then, Jan and me, reaching for the wine, on our way to the ambassador's party. The coach jolts into a track large enough to sled us; we hear ice and snow crunching under us in the dark. As the horses jerk into a gallop we shoot through squeaks and squeals where the bumpy track has been packed hard. One swallow of wine, and then to our supper in the clear, most invigoratingly cold night. The food is kept under our furs. Lise's fur was missing, naturally. And another anomaly. The strange French boy was sleeping under our furs. His pastel silks, his very white hose, clear, shining face and his curly, curly auburn hair. To touch him would have been to touch the surface of a brook. I know this feeling, I must tell it to you, how it is to reach out to the fiber of that which hopes, to touch someone whose heart believes in chance. For everyone it is different. But this boy, sleeping, smelled so strongly of our Dutch beer that I didn't touch him; I sat back and looked to Jan. "He's drunk," Jan said.

How he came to pick our coach that night I still don't know. We had our supper, riding the only good sled track between town and the ambassador's lands. Although it might have been ideal to take the sleeping celebrity home immediately, it was impossible. We would have had to turn back and ride into the lot of party-bound burghers;

we'd end up fighting beside collided coaches. "There's the Leuwens; 'parently *they* don't think it'll be a very good party," and so on. No, the course was set and I would have to appear at the ambassador's while Jan stayed with the boy in the coach. We arrived and I was in and out, speaking only to the ambassador's family. As I walked out into the cold, the cardinal was emerging from a carriage, alone in his capes. They splashed into the lamplight, so red that I tensed. The crimson rump of him, and then I was in the dark, headed for our coach. Fine snowy fields, with sledded coaches scattered in the moonlight, horses' bells twinkling. This seemed the best place to be at the moment, though there was not yet much coming and going between the coaches and the house. The moon was almost full, a little more than three-quarters. I gazed at it, walking among the carriages. Ours had pulled to a fence; the coachmen were sharing brandy under a tree. I sat on the fence and contemplated. I am no prude, but I was shocked at the boy's being so drunk. The breeze blew ice slivers from a tree branch onto my neck; I pulled up my rough fur collar. The moon's riven edge had a crimson cast, like a wound, where the darkness had cut in.

When we arrived at my house we carried the boy to our bedroom. He revived in time to undress himself, shaky, woozy, but awake. At first he didn't know who we were, and there was a bit of fear in the intensity with which he listened to our explanation of the evening. He said his name was Christian, and once he was propped up in bed he seemed to want to talk. I opened the connecting doors to the house and had some food brought. We sat up with him almost until dawn. Christian brightened, although he still gave an impression of the order of things having been tampered with. Christian was attached to the household of the prince de Condé, now traveling. He said that the prince "favored" him, and he said it in such a way as to imply that we would know what he was talking about. He woke up further, and looked around the room.

"Do you two live here all alone?" he asked.

"We prefer it," said Jan, an angel's smile on his face.

There was a little sweat forming under the curls on

Christian's forehead. He looked from his long-lashed eyes at us, then at his hands on the coverlet, then back at us; wet, brilliant eyes.

"I'm a baby drunk," he said, and he belched.

Jan and I looked at each other. I brought Christian a mug of warm cider. While handing it to him, with a stern look in my eyes, I pushed my hand softly and noncarnally through his curls, cropping them back from his forehead. He took his cider much like a man then, and said, "My friend who presented the theme with me; she has put up with a lot during the days of my visit. Condé has it that life is like a croquet game. I get to drinking like this. I take wine for the fog it puts around me. He plays with me only when he's drunk, the Condé. The ladies catch me in the gardens. The rest of the week, they talk about my soul. I have to marry the abbé's daughter." As if he were asking for a napkin, he then said, "May I stay with you for a week? I want to hide in Amsterdam until the Condé has gone home without me."

We asked him, of course, who the girlfriend was. He said he'd met her here. She lived with her father in Amsterdam. He laughed. He said the Condé made him present the theme and that made him feel like a foolish doll, so he'd asked his new friend to help him. We told him he could hide with us. It was one of those times when you are glad that you can actually *do* something in the world. He said his friend's name was Nanotte.

The next day I opened a separate room above the gallery for Christian.

In those late weeks of winter, into the early spring, I tried to keep Christian out of sight. Before the snow melted between the gargoyle's claws outside my window, though, Moenen had seen enough of Christian around the yard and on the canal to begin asking questions. So Christian was moved to Jan's quarters at Seekt's. We sheltered the refugee while he waited for word from his friend. Early in spring, we began taking Christian on visits to the Fredericks' see in the country. Jan was merry. He looked at me, and I could see his manly eyes sparkle. He started wearing the parson's old gold watch then. And he started painting the ceiling of the Fredericks' chapel, standing or lying—like Michelangelo—on a scaffold. Christian, mopping a floor in the chapel, said, "Herr Seekt said there are ways I can contact Nanotte without her father knowing; he says he'll help me."

"Have you told Seekt the identity of the Riddle of Amsterdam?" Jan asked, shouting down from his scaffold below the altar roof.

"Oh, yes," laughed Christian, his eyes crinkling up. (Jan and I often made a chorus about the girl's identity, while Christian remained elusive and amused.) Seekt was inside with the Fredericks, by their fire, and we spent the evening watching Jan paint the chapel roof. Above the altar, the roof was cone-shaped at a gentle angle. At the apex of the cone, Jan had painted a dove with lines of heavenly light penetrating from its aura into the richly detailed flora covering the dome. Jan drew animals among the leaves, peeking or staring into the chancel and altar, but he had not hidden a human being yet.

Christian told us about his talk with Seekt. He would have impressed Seekt; first with good humor, then with the laughing way he took charge of his own affairs. "I know I'll find her; I always do what I really want to do," he said. As we talked on the floor Jan occasionally reminded us to shout so that he could hear us. Soon, Christian had to whisper earnestly, because we suddenly had a visitor. A wonderful short, compact man strode into the chapel and produced three wooden juggling pins. I explained to Christian that the Fredericks kept their chapel open to wayfarers. The juggler kicked his pack into a corner and went about the sanctuary, juggling. We talked above the noise of the wooden pins slapping on the man's palms. Seekt came over before Jan was finished that night. He stood with Christian and me below the scaffold, fanning himself, and Christian thanked him for helping with Nanotte.

The juggler was juggling behind Seekt. A pin jetted high above our heads. Jan grabbed at the pin when it presented itself at his high platform, but he missed. Seekt flipped out his hand, received the pin in a bed of lace, and tumbled it right back again into the pattern of the juggler's three arcs. Then Seekt winked. "These boys need to be engaged," he said. I wondered what he meant.

At this time Jan was working on a painting in the city, a large group portrait commissioned by the city fathers, the burghers of Amsterdam. I urged Jan to paint them into a picture of Christ expelling the money changers from the temple, but he refused. He displayed the picture one day for the merchants who were depicted. It was only half-finished, with the heads painted into a charcoal cartoon. We stood in a gallery at the academy. The picture looked fine and promising and the men said so, with a few quibbles. Suddenly there appeared in the otherwise empty balcony Christian's girl from the concert, with that sublimely suggestive open breast. She stared at us, at the mayor; and the whole assembly gaped at her for a couple of seconds before she darted away. I was first out the doors to the street, where I saw her wide skirt squeezing into a coach, which then jolted into a run along the cobblestones, even before its door was closed. The driver must have had orders. That night Christian promised to shed some light on the mystery at last. Seekt had arranged for a note to be delivered, Christian said, and before that week was out Christian asked if we would entertain the Riddle of Amsterdam at my house for dinner. We invited Lise as well, since she was still in town with the ambassador's wife. All of us stood at the windows to watch the girl's coach pull up. Christian ran to open the coach door, with an elaborate bow to the boy who emerged. The boy hurried Christian inside. In the hall, Christian put his arms on the boy's shoulders and said, "This is my friend, friends. His name is Peter."

I said, "I know you! Who are you?"

"I'll tell you everything. I am so glad you have kept Christian in Amsterdam; I was so glad to hear it. You have seen me at parties, and perhaps at the concert. But to the parties I came as I am tonight—Mayor Vilbris's son, Peter." And he bowed.

Chunky, not slight. You could see that famous chest, well defined even under a light shirt. During dinner he explained what he was doing. He displayed an interesting process while he talked: Peter was but a collection of passions which conversation called up. He was bitter about his father. Vilbris had discovered him once with a stableboy on their farm, Peter said, and had had the boy whipped, making Peter watch. Recently there had been a similar story about the crown prince in the house of Hohenzollern. For revenge, Peter hit on a way of embarrassing his father mercilessly. Vilbris knew well enough, Peter said, who the provocative girl really was when Peter dressed up. Lock Peter up as Vilbris might, every time Peter escaped he did it again, coming closer and closer, Peter said, to friends of his father who might recognize him, as Lise almost had. His strength impressed me, especially looking into his finely, almost femininely speckled blue eyes. His impetuosity alarmed Jan.

"But are you provoking him too far? Is he not dangerous?" Jan asked.

"Dangerous he is. I hope I frighten him, keep him from making a family disagreement public, make him leave me alone. But so far, he seems only to get angrier. My father has read the Bible and knows that he who troubles his own house shall inherit the wind. It's lucky that Christian's note reached me. Father was making me go to school in Switzerland next week, with a horrible tutor. Will you hide me?"

"Certainly," I said to Peter. "If you two can't stay here in my house permanently, we can find you other good places."

We ate our dinner with the two refugees. Conversation was giddy and rich, of the sort from which you save delicacies to think about later. Possibilities narrowed quickly when Frederick One burst into the room and cleared out everybody but me and Jan. He told us that navy police were scouring the waterfront that night, collecting the sailors and seizing "stragglers." The stragglers were being kidnapped into the merchant service, especially onto whaling ships. Frederick had stopped to warn us. He was on his way to Seekt's house with a friend who would have to hide until they could get him into the country. He had been seen.

I asked if we could meet with Seekt tomorrow. Would Frederick ask Seekt if we could visit him the next day? We arranged that for noon, and Frederick hurried out. We saw Lise to her horse then, and we heard the two boys whistling in the rooms above us. Christian whistled out of tune, and Peter loudly helped him.

Seekt was assembling a collection of paintings for a lady of great wealth. There were some one hundred paintings and drawings of which the lady's agents had already approved. Frames hung all over the lower floor of his house. In the biggest salon, with tall windows, pictures had been hung top to bottom as in an academy. The light through the windows was clear, and lit the paintings without directly touching them. Seekt said he was particularly pleased by the lady's request for drawings. He showed me a pair of large drawings that Rembrandt van Rijn had made of a youth seated on a horse, and said they would be his gift to the lady. Seekt said he had prepared some food in the observatory on top of his house. He could not comfortably climb a ladder, so on the top floor we found an elaborate staircase, which we ascended into the glass house on the roof. The Fredericks were waiting for us under the glass. It might have been a greenhouse once. Jan had never been in it before. We sat down with the Fredericks and held mugs of beer; didn't eat very much; looked out past the harbor at the pull of the horizon on the far ocean. Jan inspected Seekt's telescope.

"You know I always wanted to bring sons here," Seekt said. "My wife couldn't have any children after Katje was born."

I watched the Fredericks that day. Both capable, both with big hands. What an initiation, I imagined, thinking of Jan, who was sitting on the black and white tile floor under the telescope.

Frederick One said, "Well, we have known the mayor's views for some time now. And the others'. But there have never been such harsh measures, only occasional clearings-off at the plage. What is happening?"

We gazed into the distance until Seekt said, "The presence of the navy means that the mayor and town council have consulted the regent. The short form of that is this: the body politic is now willing to support the mayor in his campaign against the young men, or at least to tolerate it for a time."

"What about the courts?" asked Frederick Two.

"No law is involved yet," said Seekt, "other than vagrancy, or city ordinances about 'orderliness' and such. I doubt that Vilbris would seek to prosecute homosexuals in civil courts. The cities as corporate entities have too meager a legal heritage in our system to take much initiative. No, the old clerical courts would be the place for that. Hm."

"So we have no recourse to law now?"

"None."

"But there are hundreds of boys in this city who will end as whale food soon, who have nowhere to stay," said Jan. "And we know them."

"It would be a good plan if we helped as many as we encounter," said Seekt, "while we prepare for subsequent events. We will need three carriages to encounter them in."

Seekt explained a plan for transporting evacuees to the Fredericks' chapel, and thence to some less temporary place of their choosing, if possible. Seekt and I volunteered carriages, and a wagon was to be sought. Both carriages would go the rounds of friends' houses looking for young men in trouble, and the chapel could give them sanctuary for the night. The Fredericks went quickly to the country to prepare food. We set a maximum of thirty guests for the first night.

Seekt and Jan and I remained in the observatory talking while the sky grew pink and hazy with a spring sunset. I watched gulls circling a Spanish merchantman's mast. As the breeze became a chilly wind from the sea, I was planning what legal and strategic resources I could muster.

"My twin brother is at the mayor's," I added, "where he has been assiduously friendly with men of his views and class. He means to make a presence wherever he is, I think."

Seekt was playing with a large ball of crystal. I saw the three of us, and a domino pattern of black and white tiles, reflected in the round prism. "How will he stand?" asked Seekt. "Can you tell?"

I said not. We came down from the observatory, agreeing to meet next morning at the Fredericks' see in the country.

For several weeks we were occupied with transporting young men back and forth to the Fredericks' see. With raids in town once every week or fortnight, we were often busy smuggling a fugitive or two into the long dormitory above Seekt's stables. Jan's quarters also seemed the safest place for Christian and Peter, so they moved in with Jan permanently. It was fun trying to pair off the new fugitives, give them beds near each other to add a little life to the proceedings. Sometimes we would all talk late at Jan's; the bronze chandeliers blazed far into the night. The Fredericks' place was thriving. I was told that even in this adversity, the tenants there managed to enjoy a multitude of diversions. I thought of them sleeping in the chapel, lying under Jan's ceiling at night. Maybe the two guitarists played; maybe the candles were lit.

So, suddenly, the Dutch courts and churches—the "morality" as we called it—were scouring the countryside for witches and young men. We were safe, but there were friends who had friends arrested and dragged to actual prisons with straw in cold stone cells. There had been witchcraft trials, and they burned three women at the stake. We waited for news of the first trial of a boy-lover.

Moenen I hardly saw. I passed into the full spring without a serious talk with him. I would look hard and long at him; we knew we loved each other. We never spoke of the trials. I did not want to vex him yet. In any case, I knew he could do little, being a junior adviser. I kept hoping that, when I needed him, he could help me. It wasn't time just yet.

Then, that day in May, the day which seemed inconsequential at the time, Jan and I picked up a tailor in the Leuwen carriage. We got to his house just before the city guard did, and took him to Jan's quarters until we could get him to the Fredericks'. The carriage then left me and Jan in the courtyard of my house. When we reached the downstairs door to my rooms, we paused for a time in the fine spring weather, looking at the canal, talking.

"Why was he so effeminate, Jan?"

"Why not?" replied Jan.

"Well, he was so flighty and girlish. And you encouraged him!" I complained.

"Listen, flower," he said to me, "people are made differently. If he wants to play the lady, he may. That's his right. And if he needs to do that today, when his whole life is disrupted, his home and his livelihood vanished, confiscated in an instant by brutal strangers, then we let him play and pose today. Today of all days. That is his courage, Steen. His imagination and his dignity rise up and say, 'You may step on my hem, tear my laces, smear my makeup off my face; but you cannot touch me or change me a jot; I spit on you.' Remember, in your carriage, how grand he was? That was courage. I tried to help because his life is over for a time. You always try to help anyway, unless it's a rascal. What does it cost you?"

He pulled me to him and we began to kiss very small, tender kisses. I abandoned caution, and we kissed deeply. But for some reason, all of a sudden I opened my eyes and I saw, beyond Jan's shoulder, my twin brother Moenen standing among the hedges watching us. Not watching us, exactly; Moenen's eyes were fixed that moment directly on mine, in mine, while the wind blew strands of his beautiful curly hair around his face. As I held on to Jan, Moenen reamed me with his eyes, his face set like a statue's. Then he turned and glided away.

Then came the day in June when I visited Christian and Peter at Jan's studio. Peter had communicated with his father, assuring him that he was well and that he loved him. I realized that Peter was as fanatical as his father. On this one June day I brought them bad news. Contrary to Seekt's guess, the city fathers had put in the law courts a case involving a teacher arrested on the plage during the first raids. The lawyers ended, I was told, trying the case on "moral" grounds of some kind; witchcraft had been discussed. The court, I had to tell Christian and Peter at the studio that day, condemned the teacher to be burned as a witch.

But Peter already knew, and he knew that it was to take place that afternoon, a fact I'd omitted. We were frightened. I cannot describe exactly the sense I had of this; to be peaceable, and to stand in the light of day among one's kind, and to be told that what you are is wrong. I know no parallel. The court's ruling said of the teacher, "Your nature is debased and your kind are an abomination." He was said to be a good teacher.

I believe most thoughtful people in Amsterdam were dismayed that day. Christian and Peter both wanted to go and see the burning. I went to the square with them. We stood under a shoemaker's arch of white stucco. The pyre, in the center of the square, was a heap of straw and sticks, roughly conical. When they led the man out he was hooded, hands tied. Because he could not see to balance himself, he stumbled behind them. Someone said he was a botanist at the university, and that he had been well respected by his students. He began to resist as they dragged him onto the sticks, his body going rigid and his feet digging in. They lifted him and heaved his body to the top like a sack. As he was being roped to the stake, he jerked and threw himself away from it with all his might, throwing himself, mute, into their arms. They tied his head back. Silence throttled each of us, and then there was the popping and crackling of the wood in flames. They couldn't see each other, but Peter and Christian were both watching this with incredible hatred knotting their faces. We pushed our way out of the square as, finally, the teacher made a noise. He was choking like a baby; it sounded like he couldn't get any air. The crowd remained silent.

Moenen came home that night and I wanted to know what he intended to do. He spoke first.

"Today I was appointed a judge on the civil court," he announced. I longed for him, then, to be my champion.

"How will you vote if one of those insane cases comes to you?" I asked.

"I must obey the law," he said.

"If politics has made you so thirsty for legality, must I expect to be burned soon?" I asked.

He looked at me with bitterness then, and I didn't know why. His fair, still-young features contorted in a grimace, and he looked away. "We are never harmed, Brother. The awful thing is that there is no control of the crowds. They have seized prisoners, as you know. I am going up to see Mother."

I watched him climb the stairs, and realized that he seemed much older than I, of a different generation somehow, as strange and unsympathetic as some figure you bump into on the street. I hated it.

The next month, Moenen was one of the judges in the case of an apothecary who lived with another man. They passed the letter of the law, in some fashion. Outside the court, the mob took the apothecary and tore him apart at the joints, using four horses. But I thought, even at that time, that my life was safe.

CHAPTER FOUR

ALTHOUGH the beast of human affairs had turned its fangs toward us, I did not sense personal disaster. I looked at my sumptuous rooms; I looked at the unlined grace of Peter's and Christian's faces at night. I sensed eternity. It seems a natural vision when I look into the face of a young boy or girl. I seek to look at them for just that illusion; here the shriveling step of the unthinkable is halted. Come, give me your smile. It cannot happen here.

So while we watched developments and helped friends escape the persecution, we simply hoped that it would be over soon, run itself out. We were fairly joyous together, really. It was a romantic time—our escapes to the see; we were heroes on midnight rides through the warm spring nights. You know how the air of a spring evening is both warm and cool at once, warm especially in the heavy odors from blooms invisible in the dark. We rode through tides of growing things, taking fugitives to safety, Jan and I, then rode home to our bed.

Who knows heaven before it is gone? What angel, leaving space and the weak clouds of spring and the subtle heartbeat of the stars behind forever, does not sigh through his tears, Ah, had I only known! Forgive me, but this next part is the most difficult.

To begin with, Jan had taken a strange commission that spring. He was to finish a memorial statue, just supervise the final casting, for the cathedral here in Amsterdam. The rich archdiocese, of mostly Spanish prelates and almost no faithful left among the Dutch, took it as a point of pride to finish a commemorative statue which had been planned during the last days of Spanish influence. It was an equestrian monument of Philip II, the last of the great Spanish Hapsburgs, who had sent out the armada against Elizabeth of England. He was the last ruler of the Spanish empire to have held real sway in Holland. As a point of pride, the archdiocese wanted this Spanish emperor memorialized on his horse before their cathedral, in a square shared by a large Dutch Reformed church as well as by the town hall. The cardinal, who was of course in charge, felt that anti-Spanish feeling had diminished sufficiently that he could see the thing done in his lifetime. When the academy recommended Jan for the final casting, the cardinal accepted. Jan did not demur either because, as he told me, he would gladly take some Spanish gold so they might no longer have the use of it. The casting was not difficult to oversee, since the molds had already been prepared. By April the thing was ready for the empty pedestal in front of the cathedral.

At the final meeting, Jan made a strange request. An abbot handed him a bag of doubloons. After counting them out on the table, Jan shoved back a pile of the shining gold—exactly half of the amount. To the shocked abbot, Jan said that he would take only half the sum if they would let him stand upon the pedestal at the unveiling and would introduce him to the crowd as the man who had finished the piece. After some confusion, the abbot agreed. Jan explained to me that it would help him to be known to the people. "But Spain, and that church, are still pretty unpopular," I argued. "Why identify yourself with them?" He winked at me, giving no answer beyond that.

The archdiocese had planned their unveiling for Easter morning, so that it would take place in the middle of the Easter procession that converged in the square. An arrogant piece of timing, but guaranteeing lots of spectators. Easter morning was cool and beautiful, and the square was thronged with people who had come early to witness the children's procession that wound in from the countryside. Each Easter the children walked into the city, or rode in carts, carrying flowers and leading sheep. Before the procession arrived, the bells of the cathedral began to toll, announcing the end of their mass.

The crowd around me grew attentive as the priests, mass said, appeared in the cathedral doors and formed ranks on the wide stairs above the statue. At the same time, Jan climbed up onto the pedestal. He would soon pull away the cloth and reveal the statue. As the cardinal took his place in front of the priests, high on the stairs above the square, a priest began to announce the unveiling. He got little attention until Jan held up his arms for silence. The priest eulogized Philip II, and while he did, Jan began lounging in the most ludicrous way against the veiled monument, posing. There was laughter. The clerics could not see Jan from their position behind the statue. When it came to his own name as "native author" of the work, Jan held up his arms for silence again. The words "Jan of Soest, sculptor" were shouted out by the priest, and Jan took such a ridiculous bow that the whole crowd began to laugh and hoot. Then the priest's speech was done, and the cathedral bells boomed in the tower. The procession entered the square, singing a surly laud, led by an enormous wagon filled with children holding flowers and weeds.

The cardinal looked at them. The sunlight was brilliant on their heads and faces as the multitude of children, cleanly dressed, dragged into the square. As their wagon drew near the statue, Jan pulled the cloth. It tumbled down like a white carpet on which the children might ride. In the shafts of morning sun, the statue smote our eyes with a burst of light. The ancient bells in the tower above clanged and boomed, drowning everything. Then, as the wagon reached the far side of the statue, just beneath the bell tower, one of the bells broke loose and, trailing its ropes and crosspiece, hurtled down toward the stairs fronting the cathedral. Above the screaming of the crowd you could see and hear, oddly, the clapper smash against the bell's sides as it flipped through the air. The wagon halted, its horses shying. The children caught the panic of the crowd without even noticing, most of them, the catastrophe hurtling through the air toward them. I watched Jan in those long instants, and saw that he knew one thing to try and was going to risk it. The instant the bell broke loose, he'd begun rocking the statue back and forth in the wet mortar on its pedestal, rocking with the whole force of his body. By inches at first, the heroic horse and rider rocked laterally toward the stairs, then back again. The bell crashed onto the top stairs. The priests drew back—all but the cardinal. He gazed at this throughout, not budging, crimson capes billowing. The clapper came loose, and the bell bounded high in the air. Jan chose this moment, and rocked the statue off its base directly into the arc of the bell. Philip II crushed the bell on the empty stairs behind the pedestal, making a shuddering, sharp peal like the crack of doom.

The children were frightened out of their wits and ran screaming to be embraced in the crowd. All that was left was a wagonful of flowers, and blossoms strewn around the empty pedestal. Above the noise of the children, you could hear the repeated cheers, "Jan the sculptor, Jan the sculptor." He had jumped down. I ran to him, and as I hugged him I was bathed in sweat from his chest and back. Above us, on the stairs, the Spanish cardinal peered down his long hooked nose at us, his crimson capes billowing in the fitful winds of spring.

The next week, Katje and Lise arrived home together. Lise had quit the ambassador's service; she would stay in Seekt's household. As for Katje, I think Seekt was lonely for his daughter; I think he wanted her near him, and that he persuaded her to leave her viscomte and return to Amsterdam. It felt like the arrival of fresh allies on the field of battle. Jan and I sat with the girls at Seekt's dinner table one night, while Seekt described the persecutions as the product of a fervor in the churches and the councils to restore the stability of a country whose greatness they imagined to be slipping away. Holland still traded over all the oceans, with colonies in the Far East and the Americas, but since the deterioration of the navy we could no longer assume one of the commanding roles in the concert of Europe, and we had to follow policies set in other capitals. Louis XIV's last war, to place his grandson on the throne of Spain, had left our land army and defenses a shambles. There was a reaction, and reaction took the form of trying to rid the country of elements seen as licentious, useless, or unorthodox. Though Catholics were not persecuted, the small sects were, and it was dangerous not to belong to the Reformed Church. Witches made a spectacular target, and they were seized upon early, as were the young men who had always congregat-

MY BROTHER'S IMAGE

ed in the taverns and boardinghouses near the waterfront. When Seekt described some of the recent executions and the instances of mob justice, the girls were incredulous. Katje looked through the candlelight at Jan and me for a moment, and before she lowered her eyes I blushed.

One night, Katje visited Jan in his quarters. He told me about it the next day; we shared most things. I will tell you how their visit went. Jan was working late at night in his studio at the end of the long gallery. He was alone, no fugitives present. The low-set windows were open to new spring smells, the wet earth giving up its winter dead. Suddenly Jan noticed a draft flickering the candlelight as darkness jumped here and there on his canvas. He turned and saw the studio door opening. There is that night hour when your pulse races at such things, and Jan felt feathers rushing up his legs and back. He stared at the door as Katje walked in. She was dressed plainly, as usual, her long golden hair falling onto a dark dress. On seeing Jan's stare, she laughed a little, cocking her head to one side. Jan sighed. His big shoulders relaxed. He looked at her sheepishly.

"Scared of me?" asked Katje.

"No," he said quickly. "No . . ." Their eyes met for an instant, and hers looked into his as though asking several questions at once. "No. But of the wind, yes. Katje! The candles go out." His head cocked too as they relaxed, gazed at each other. "The light flickers among the ghosts in my drawings, their outlines dim; I turn and the door is slowly stealing open toward me; the breeze grows colder . . ."

"Stop!" Katje said, louder than she meant to. Both laughed in the candlelight. Katje was shivering; she hugged her shoulders tightly, arms crossed over her breast. Jan had good manners; he did not go over and calm her with a familiar hug. That would have been indecent, possibly premature. Instead he saw her shivering and said, "Ah," in a tone that warmed her, or permitted her to warm herself. The voice can do that, especially a voice as full in the chest as his.

"Come sit," he said, motioning to the chair opposite his easel, which was warmed a little by the light of the candles on the table there. She leaned on the edge of the chair, rubbing her fists up and down her thighs, looking at his picture. Looking, she absentmindedly drew a long silk kerchief from her bodice and tied it over her shoulders. Had there not been such intelligence in the angle of her eyes and the attention on her face, she would have looked as though she possessed everything.

"What is this a study for?" she asked, looking at him then as if he might not answer her.

It was Jan's turn to be surprised. "Why, ah, it's a study for my picture of the city fathers. Though I loathe them now, I am a professional, and I will finish it. I've been paid. Everything is done but their shoes, and I also need to arrange the heroic, but tamed and obedient, sea winds sweeping the balcony. Those are Dutch merchantmen on the horizon, of course. Can you see our flag, that long wisp under the cloud? I . . ." He stopped, gazing at her and breathing. As he paused, she recrossed her arms so her hands again rested on her shoulders and smiled at him as at a child, ruefully.

"Jan." Serious business now. "I heard what you did on Sunday in the square." She paused, and both of them looked gravely childlike for an instant. "Are you trying to get killed? What were you trying to do?"

"Well, at first I just wanted to mock the cardinal's stupid ceremony. And I wanted to make some kind of good name with the crowd, as self-defense, in case I need it someday. Steen has his family and money. I thought I could help my position by making myself popular with a little clowning. But I didn't plan the heroics—that bell was an act of God, I swear."

"Was the statue smashed beyond repair?" she asked.

"Completely."

"All in all, Jan, the cardinal must hate you." Jan nodded, looking aside as if he'd tasted bad fish. "And what worse enemy could you have? The cardinal can deal as he likes with his enemies now, my father says. Worse, he has an excuse: he must know about you and Steen. He may not go after Steen, but surely the writ is already drawn for you, Jan. What are you going to do?"

"Well, I can finish the city fathers tomorrow, you see. That's why I'm working here. I plan to take this cartoon in at dawn tomorrow, finish the painting and then ride to your father's place in the country to stay with the Fredericks. It has been safe there so far. We've trained the boys for self-defense against all but the army itself, and there are cellars to hide in if worst comes to worst. So I'll be out of town for a while."

"All right," she said, "but . . . why did you risk it, Jan? Risk such a display?"

He said, "I don't know," and looked far past her, through the window.

As he went to pour wine into glasses, she leaned back in her chair, sighing in her nose so that he wouldn't hear it. She wanted to cry, and therefore took the glass of wine from him with her head averted. The effect must have made her seem abstracted. Jan, turning back to his sketch, said, "It was so nice." He stood with his back to her and sipped from his glass while she rubbed her cheek against the wing of the chair. It was luxurious for her not to ask what Jan meant.

"You haven't told me about your meeting with Steen the first time. The first time, you know, when I'd sent him to you," Katje said into the dark of the room.

For reply, Jan shifted his weight and shook his head a couple of times. He half turned to her, giving only his profile really, looking at the wine he was swirling in his glass. "It was very nice."

"Did you seduce him?" Katje asked, curling her legs under her. "Did he seduce you?"

Jan's head bobbed back and forth as he followed the whirlpool he'd created in his glass. "A little of both," he finally said, "mostly me, I guess."

Katje still looked away from him. "Did you kiss him?"

Jan jerked his big eyes at her, alarmed, until he realized that this was a sophisticated conversation, that she was from Versailles. He smiled, and although it embarrassed him, he said, "Not right away, no." Then, during the pause, he realized that she was not able to ask another question, so he said, "I told him you said he should model for me."

Katje smiled. Lazily, she said, "And you posed him as a young god, and while his face was fixed, staring at the ceiling, you came and kissed him. Did you?"

"No," Jan murmured. He finished his wine in a gulp and moved toward Katje's chair, his heart suddenly so full of sympathy that his mind fell years back into his past, to his family. As he approached Katje, he could see only the dirt yard in front of his parents' house, and his mother bending over him and Lise to give them cool water. His mother's skirts rustled in the sun around them; she gave them the cool drink and was gone. Lise lifted her round head of curls to him and Lise's face giggled—little, round, fat face, only a few teeth in her baby mouth as she giggled at him, eyes laughing, and spit ran down her chin. Lise raised her pudgy arm to touch his face, twisting the hand so oddly in reaching, as babies do, and instead of knuckles she had tiny indentations in her fat hand. The sun flashed. There were only the baby giggles, as Jan said, "No, I didn't kiss him. You see, there is a screen for undressing. Come here, now." He lifted Katje from the chair, and she looked up at him with welcome interest and some surprise. "Back here," he said, leading her. Before she went behind the screen she looked at him as if at a statue that had moved. He was naked when she came out. She was wearing her shift. Her flesh was full, shining, as she ran her finger down the muscles of his arm, watching him. He turned to her and rubbed his hand on the back of her neck. He said, "Did you know about Steen being in love with you?"

"No," she said, and Jan put his mouth to hers. Both their bodies were very hot.

"Yes," he said, as they were kissing, "somebody died, and you were beautiful, so he needed you, and you went away."

"No, no," she said. He undid her shift, and after it fell his hands smoothed her breasts.

"Yes," he said, "somebody." Maybe they sank to their knees. I guess the silent breeze that blew along the floor smelled of new wet buds and of the earth giving up its winter dead.

Early dawn after his night with Katje found Jan in the cavernous, gray, and silent academy, where he stood before his group portrait of the burghers of Amsterdam. As he stood dwarfed in front of the canvas, the high, mullioned windows dusted gray-purple light on him in the hush of the large flagstone studio. All was nearly completed, their arrogant faces staring from the pose at haughty angles, heads thrown back, necks hard. A few stared attentively at one another; one or two looked curiously away to something at the sides, but, in the main, each man thought about his own destiny. Some wore black broad-brimmed hats, some held them carelessly at their sides; there was a rich profusion of white lace and white ribbons decking necks and chests. Their eyes, all big and glassy and bold, seemed to look within. In each dark iris was a conquered self. So they stared down self-sufficient profiles at the viewer. They do to this day, hanging over the stairs in the town hall and making visitors feel unworthy to climb farther. Maps, a globe, batons, and books lie around them like discarded toys. But Jan did one thing I love in this: the face at center-most in the group—a fine, contemplative man seated in rich robes—wears an expression that, while proud, is still unutterably sad, one eyebrow raised, as he gazes into space from among them all.

So, Jan slashed with his brush a few more times that morning in the empty light. The shine was caught onto the richness of their silks, the sea wind tamed among the window drapes. Their buckles gleamed in elegant disorder. One detail he thought they lacked. He dipped his brush in black and, throwing aside his palette, putting on his hat, Jan went to the canvas, heels cracking on the stone flags. A scroll was visible to the fore of the group, held negligently in the mayor's left hand, a blank scroll. Onto the scroll Jan dashed some words in large Gothic lettering. Then he threw back his head, took it all in, and turned his back on the picture forever. As he strode from the hall toward his horse in the courtyard below, heels hard on the cold stone flags, the reddening light of morning leaked and leaked into the room, gradually bringing up the curves and angles of the letters drying on the mayor's parchment scroll. To this day, viewers squint and read:

Faith, Hope, and . . .

Jan rode straight to the Fredericks' see that morning, taking care to avoid the corners and roads where there usually were sentries—with one exception. He did use the city gate under which he had passed with Seekt that early morning long ago, in the black and gold carriage with the roan horse behind. He slowed his horse so that, passing under the arch, he could take the horse at a proud, high-stepping walk, *clop, clop* echoing off the walls. For this he took off his plumed hat and held it at his side. Then he spurred hard, and galloped away.

My own part of that day began quietly. Peter and Christian had slept in Christian's old room at my house, and when I woke alone in my big bed that morning, I knew Jan was already on the road to the see. Odd, reflective morning for me, it was. I felt like the senior partner, or a chaperon, with the two young boys sleeping together next door. I was, maybe, a year older than they, but because Jan was my lover, and because we harbored them, I felt much older. As I folded my arms behind my head, sinking into the long linen pillows, the bed seemed a sea of sheets, too big without Jan. I was surprised at this. "Do not endow with any romance any unromantic thing," I said into the dark damask-and-pewter-and-silver room I had made. Gray light swelled through the window frames. The rich woods of the walls and mantel glimmered as if I had never been there at all, as if ages before and after would savor them and I were only a disembodied voyeur. Soon the air grew warm and bright, reminding me that yellows and greens were blooming outside; and then birds piped up, filling the morning with their clipped salutes. I listened. No, the boys were not awake yet. I lay still. Soon my brain was swelling with essays of revenge: I would kidnap Moenen, I would confront the mayor. But I realized that I had better talk with Seekt first. I would be good about this, mature. I would get up, make breakfast for us all, feed the boys, visit my mother; and then ride like hell for the see after Jan.

I rose and dressed. Passing the boys' door, I marched straight down the long hall of the upper gallery to the doors connecting us to the house. I unlocked and threw them open so hard that they banged against the walls. On to the upper landing of the house I strode, and down the great staircase, shouting, "Who's about? Who's about!" I clapped my hands at each step. Servants ran out into the hall, staring at me, shrinking back as I descended. By the time I reached the hall a party of six servants was cowering against the doorway, afraid I had a fever or something. When I confronted them, all the bravado left me at once and I wondered what I had been doing. But I had to continue to glare like a tyrant. I didn't dare let my eyes shrink back to normal size or my chest fall back in place. "Good morning," I announced. I didn't mean to pause there, but a breath's time was enough for their ragged, precipitate, "Good morning, sir." I acknowledged that with what I thought was a fitting dip of the head. Still, they stared. Then, without having planned this, I said, "May I have breakfast for three? Three." Throwing my voice at any twin who might be eavesdropping from above, I finished, "In my rooms, please."

"Yes, sir," they answered, bowing or curtsying as if they were in a play.

Stunned at the cogency of my own request, I dipped my head again. "Thank you," I said. "Hette," I said to the mute kitchen girl, "will you serve it, please?" She reddened. When I smiled at her, she did not relax. I dipped my head again, turning to mount the stairs. "Three!" I shouted as I began to climb, flinging the word like a gauntlet. I climbed the staircase very firmly, hearing Hette pace away downstairs, but as I rounded the top I saw no one waiting there. So I threw a defiant puff of the chest toward the empty hallway, then strode through the connecting doors. I left them slightly ajar behind me.

I had just gotten the boys into chairs around the table in my room when I heard Hette's knock on the double doors at the other end of the hall. Peter and Christian were wearing nightgowns, so I had to shout, *Three!* again in my mind. Then I went to my door and shouted down the long reach of the hall, "Come in!"

Both doors swung back from Hette's kick to reveal her standing with a huge tray. She almost lost her balance because our big, sloppy St. Bernard, who likes me, pushed past her and bounded down the hall toward me. Feet scratching and skidding on the waxed tiles, he leaped along, slobbering, growing larger and larger in the square white perspective of that hall. Then in one jump he was upon me, paws on my shoulders. I banged on his sides the way he enjoys, then led him back down the hall, pulling on his collar. We almost collided with the burdened Hette, who squeezed past us holding the enormous tray over our heads. As I closed the dog into the house, I realized she was by then serving the boys. *Three!* I shouted in my mind.

That was a pleasant breakfast. The food was nice, not the usual fare I burned on my stove; some fruits and bread and a delicious coffee. The morning air was warm and bright through the windows, and the boys smiled at each other, at me. I explained that Jan had had to go to the country, for safety's sake. We became somber, too jaded for Eden, the three of us. They wanted to start out immediately and join Jan, but I persuaded them to go and fetch Lise and bring her along too in a coach later that afternoon. They agreed to this, and soon set off for Seekt's house to explain to Lise. They would borrow a carriage from Seekt, and I cautioned them to hitch a single horse for each of them to the sides of the carriage in case anything went wrong or they were stranded somewhere. We were careful about things, you see.

I cleared our breakfast, then locked the double doors again and left by my private stairway as the boys had done. I selected the best horse in our stables and paced him very smartly through the streets of Amsterdam. My eyes darted with a curious regard at the houses, canals, and squares of my city. I began to feel myself a stranger, and I wondered who were these people who were causing us so much trouble? What sort of place was this? If acquaintances saw me that morning they must have wondered at me, riding by everything slowly and intently.

In the late afternoon I reached the see, where I dropped my sedate disposition immediately and rushed to the chapel looking for Jan. I don't know why I picked the chapel, but as I halted in the open door I knew I'd been right. Late afternoon light made the place rosy, the very stones giving off an ancient tint. Shadows gathered in the corners, but the rose and golden light of the spring outside still filled the air, buoying the dust motes that danced and swirled in direct shafts of sun from the windows. The air held an unusual gift of warmth. I leaned in the doorway looking at Jan. He stood on top of a high ladder, holding a big palette, painting on the dome above the altar. I watched his muscles strain a little at the work, reaching, working quickly, and it seemed that here, as I watched him without his knowing it, was one of our most intimate times. I felt a closeness, a peace with him that I could trust entirely. I watched him working alone in the last light, watched until he stopped to admire his work. Then I made a cough, like the cough of a stranger who has interrupted something, and paced into one of the shafts of direct sunlight. As I stood in the light he climbed down the ladder quickly and walked to me without a word. He embraced me, holding me tightly against him for a long time, breathing. Then he held me away from him for a minute, looked at me, and said, "What's the matter? Are you tired of the pleasures of the city?" My eyes stayed fixed in his as I nodded. Then we kissed.

"Let's go for a walk!" he said, calling over his shoulder as he passed through the shafts of sunlight to put his ladder away. I followed him, and as he stowed the ladder I saw what he had done in the dome. That forest beneath the rays of the dove looked complete, and now, beside the animals and green things, Jan had put a man—a man sleeping naked against the trunk of a tree. The man's face was cradled on his hands, the front of his body almost falling from the dome toward the viewer. I gazed at it, still staring as Jan came and put his arm around my shoulders. Jan had copied my own features for the man's face.

We walked out of the chapel into the warm dusk. Neither of us spoke. We didn't even hold hands. There was a physical presence to our not touching. The earth, too, was consumed with itself, its smells and wetness sinking into it again and again. Our whole tour of the Fredericks' see was accomplished in complete silence, although we never agreed to keep silent. From the chapel, we walked among men and boys and young women hurrying to the Fredericks' house to prepare dinner. Some were left finishing the piling of the last terra-cotta tiles for the chapel roof. A girl carried an apronful of potatoes from a storehouse toward the kitchen. They were mostly young, a few middle-aged men and women too, coming in from the fields with hoes and pieces of dismantled plows over their shoulders, finished with the day's planting. Far in the distance, where the horizon made one line of the field on our left, two tiny figures led a team of oxen to the barn, inclined at an angle to the earth as they pulled the beasts along. Closer against that horizon, a silhouette with a broad-brimmed hat rode a team of slow, plodding dray horses.

In fields that bordered the state road, Jan and I marched parallel to lines of earthworks that gangs were digging up, smoothing into long mounds. These, I guessed, were for defense; I had heard that there was musket practice regularly now at the see. Two boys with sweaty faces looked up at us out of their trench and made low, sweeping bows, brushing imaginary hats in the dirt. Our eyes met, and I laughed with them. The walk ended on a serious note as we neared the house. From there, fresh sentries for the night were striding toward the borders of the farm, real muskets over their shoulders, to replace the day guard. My pulse raced.

We found both Fredericks in the kitchen, among steaming pots of various things, and asked them where dinner was served. They directed us back outside, to a stand of elm trees near the house. There we found five long tables set on trestles, candles burning in Chinese lanterns set down the length of them. By now Jan and I were keeping silent together, like one organism. That sunset, we still spoke not a word to each other. But when we sat down at one table, he at the head and I to his left, we smiled at each other, looking in each other's eyes a long time. The red sun lost its battle with the little lanterns among the black trunks of the trees. Jan and I turned to watch the rest of the fugitives coming into the circle of light to have their meal. They came mostly in twos, which was humorous and buoyed me. Occasionally, parties of a few people arrived; these usually consisted of one older man or woman among a group of youths, all talking, teasing. One man with prematurely white hair in such a group suddenly turned in the direction of the dark fields, cupped his hands to his mouth, and yodeled so deeply and loudly that my heart raced and my ears hurt. I could not believe such a noise could come from a human throat. Smiling, a girl who seated herself opposite me explained, "That's our dinner bell."

Plates were brought from the house. Steaming serving

dishes were placed among the lanterns. All the tables were well filled with diners. As the Fredericks brought the last of the food, warm bread on long trays, all were seated and talk died down. Silent people cast glances at those still making noise. In roughly the center of this gathering, ringed by solid, dark tree trunks, a figure rose. The flickering candlelight showed a formidable woman with a manly haircut swept under an expensive ribbon, a sprig of holly stuck in her hair. Her large frame seemed not fat, but hulking, big breasted. On her large, muscled arm was one plain gold bracelet, visible when she rested her fist on the table, waiting for silence, glancing sharply from side to side. She cleared her throat like a very well-respected schoolteacher, and worked her chin back and forth once. As complete silence fell, a steady breeze could be heard visiting the circle of trees, a little cold now. The lady looked sharply into the canopy of branches and the patch of stars, and shouted, "Lord, we've come from many different places—most of us because we had to, some of us because we desired to. The reason we're here, they tell us, is that You hate us. But we don't believe that. They tell us we are Your mistakes. We don't believe You make mistakes. Many of us are young, God. Remember us who are young, in our goings out and in our comings in.

"Now we are going to partake of the rich variety of Your earth and sustain ourselves. We give You thanks for the rich variety of Your created world. For the spirits You are, growing and nourishing as You are, man or woman, Lord, we give thanks. You are our home, Lord. Preserve us who are Yours alone."

The meal was lively; jokes and tickling and pinching and passing of dishes and kissing and eating and drinking and shouts and the banging of pewter mugs on wood. Dogs leaped high in the air for bones and didn't miss. Our faces took on an eerie, ruddy glow from the candles and wine and beer. It seemed for a moment that each face was so much itself, so laughingly full of itself that we were all gods of different kinds feasting there in the ring of black trees. Hackles ran up and down my spine when, in the far dark, a bagpipe moaned and shrilled. All fell silent at the windblown, keening sound, looking that way until the piper walked from the dark, passing down the rows of tables, wailing his song, pausing for drinks. At the end of the meal the Fredericks began to supervise the clearing of the tables. Amid that confusion, Jan took me to one of the wide tree trunks, where we leaned, brushed by the cool edges of the breeze. "Let's go for a walk," he whispered.

"Will you paint yourself into the dome?" I asked.

"Come on," he said, leading me by the hand onto the furrowed field.

We walked, silent, down one furrow, I behind Jan, toward a stand of holly bushes beside the field. I knew they were hollies because, when we reached them, my bare feet felt the sharp points of the leaves. He led me to the clearing in the center of the bushes, where there was a carpeting of grass, and I looked up at the dome of the velvet sky, all silvery stars, no moon yet. The only way to be really warm was to hold each other, but as I grasped his big body I was afraid; to this day I don't know why I was afraid. I trembled until I held him harder. To calm myself, I said into his chest, "Lise and Peter and Christian should be here by now."

"Hey, flower," he said, and after an instant he pulled off his shirt. We got completely naked.

As he lay on top of me I looked past him at the silent, ceaseless pulsebeat of the stars which, when I turned my face to meet his kiss, all raced into streaks of light across the sky. Suddenly, just rubbing up against me, he began to give little cries, like sobs from deep down somewhere. I said, "Hey!" because I wasn't ready yet. But it didn't take long, and I came too before he was finished. Still he pushed himself against me, holding me; and it was only then that I noticed the sharp jab of the holly leaves buried in the grass where they stuck into my back, my arms, my legs. So I cried too.

We walked back to the chapel, holding hands. Pallets were spread waiting there. I saw two empty places under the dome when we walked in. Tall candles burned in the center of the floor, and by their light I saw figures sleeping under their blankets, a few curled up alone, mostly pairs holding—or sleeping against—each other. We stripped and lay down, then hugged for a while. When we went to sleep, he formed the front of his body along my back, our legs bent at the knees, in a sort of S shape. Our contours fit exactly, and he laid one big arm over my chest, his hand under my chin. I turned my head and whispered, "You taught me to sleep like this." But he was asleep. When I looked up, I saw the man with my face, my hair, falling toward me through the shadows.

The next thing I knew, Peter was shaking me, stocky Peter, his face solemn in the dim candle glow. It was still night. Jan was no longer beside me on the pallet. "Come!" he said. I rose, gathered up my cloak, and staggered out of the chapel behind him. In the vacant moonglow in the carriage drive outside, shivering, I listened to Peter. Christian joined us, his dark curls wet with sweat.

Peter said, "At Seekt's, when we were leaving, the cardinal's men came. His livery. Ten of them."

"More," said Christian.

"They must have had a spy in Seekt's house. They held us down while they lifted Lise onto one of their horses. We tried, we *did*, but they got her. She fought, but they had her hands tied in no time. I got my dagger and stabbed one of them in the mouth, then I stabbed the one holding Christian. Before they could grab us again we were up on the single horses and away. We knew the jumps at the stable gates; they didn't. But looking back, I saw the ones who weren't chasing us form a party around Lise and ride off."

"Where is Jan?" I said.

"I told him first," said Christian. "He went for his horse. He was gone before I could come and wake you."

"Wake the Fredericks. Stay here until I send for you. Stay here! I'm going to town." I knew I could never catch Jan before he reached town.

As I raced down the country road under the moon, the wind had fingers of ice. Before dawn, smoke rose from the chimneys of the inn where I had stopped for lunch on my way to the see the day before. Approaching fast down the road, I wouldn't have made out the smoke except that the sky was so deeply blue, rather than black, in that last of the night, the coldest hour. I noticed the thicker puffs of gray-black rising from the dark shape of the building. Nearing, I saw sparks pop occasionally from the top of the chimney. As I rounded the bend, I saw two large, smoldering fires set on either side of the road just before the gate of the inn. A figure ran into the center of the road, waving a torch. As I reined in, I saw other figures, solid dark ghosts, and a barrier too high for a horse to jump. I brought the animal around just in time to avoid a collision. He reared once, but I controlled him, and shouted down to the man, "What do you want?"

Two of them ran to me and grabbed at my horse's head, restraining me. "Who are you?" they cried, ignoring my question completely. It infuriated me.

"Steen van Leuwen," I shouted.

"Likely!" snorted the torchbearer.

Here I thought it appropriate to flourish the gold handle of my riding crop so that it sparkled in his light. At least he knew my name. That was encouraging.

"Can you prove it?" the torchbearer asked.

"Prove what?"

"You're a van Leuwen."

"I've never had to prove it." I began to spur the horse with little touches so he jumped and plunged, making the trolls sweat a little.

"What do we have to do, pull down your drawers and look for your monograms? Huh?" He thrust the torch uncomfortably close to my face, my hair. "Huh? Nice blond fire that would make, too, huh?"

I stopped kicking the horse. This was an occasion for tact. "You are militia, I see. Correct?" I said, leaning down and thrusting the torch arm aside with my shoulder, peering into his unshaven face.

"Militia, my lord. Oh, yes," he sneered.

"Then you must have a neighbor of mine for your commander. I'll bet you a sovereign he's sleeping in the inn there, isn't he?"

"Not to be disturbed before his breakfast, my lord," was the reply.

Praying they would not murder me there for my purse, I fingered a gold piece from my pocket and said, very privately, into the man's ear, palming the coin to him, "That's to wake him. Another when you tell me he's up. When he knows it's me, he'll thank you."

It worked. My horse was still restrained, but the spokesman was off to the inn. As I waited I felt my impatience and marveled at how quickly I had twisted the situation. I was perishing to ask, Anyone else pass this way? but swallowed that for the time being. Instead, I asked the shivering figures, "Why the barricade?"

"Council's orders," said a boy my age, strutting to my side. "We're blocking the roads to that queer farm down the way. Hell of a thing an hour ago. One of them, big fellow. I didn't know they made them like that. He crashed in here, waking us all. That's my brother lying in the ditch over there. Killed him. One blow of the arm, one blow. We fell back, I can tell you."

"Did the man get away?" I asked without heeding how it sounded.

"You try it, pretty boy. You should have seen him. My brother; it'll kill my folks. The monster queer, he'd have had *you* down in a shot." He raised his arm to strike me, so quickly that I recoiled. Then he laughed—a lost, nervous laugh, laughing at nothing, pretending he was laughing at me. I gave him a gold coin and watched the sneer on his face turn inward as he took it and hurried into the shadows. I was thrilled and proud for Jan, and I was furious to get back on the road after him. Even through all that, I sensed it wasn't the boy's brother in the ditch.

The torchbearer returned, picking up his torch from its place on the barricade. He said I could go into the inn to meet their captain. I asked him to water my horse.

Their captain was a renter of ours, a son of what, in ages past, would have been called a vassal. He awaited me before the fire in the hall wearing a greatcoat and nightgown. He tried to make of his men, and of my delay, a joke we could enjoy together. I didn't explain why I had chosen this route, just said I was due in town, definitely, by dawn. He didn't detain me even for a drink together. He sped me on my way, rushing out into the courtyard to order the barricade cleared for me.

"That other one didn't need it cleared, did he? *He* rode around it," mumbled the torchbearer.

Suddenly I was riding into the infinite blue of dawn. I saw the boy standing by the ditch. As I passed, he shouted a gap-toothed laugh at me, and kicked the corpse a vicious kick.

I knew Jan would head for the scene of the crime, so I

rode directly to Seekt's house. I was not prepared for what I found. There was a bivouac fire by his drive and though it was not yet eight o'clock, a small crowd waited opposite. They kept their distance because a party of French soldiers stood guard at the gate, an officer smartly in charge. As I rode up, people in the crowd shouted, "Give us the boys!" or "Want a boy? Got *one* already!" At that, my heart sank into my bowels. I rode to the officer. "I'm Steen van Leuwen," I said.

"Pass," he said, and two white-coated French guards pushed the gate.

I imagined hard, imagining Jan seated at breakfast with Seekt and Katje. I bounded up the stairs into the empty, echoing hall. I heard only my breathing, and clocks ticking. Clocks. I made for the dining room, a mausoleum; through that I ran to the morning room, bright with yellow sun. I could have sworn it came up just as I entered. Seekt stood at the windows with his back to me. Katje looked up from the table.

"Tell me," I panted.

Seekt, still facing the window, said, "We'll fix it, Steen, we'll fix it."

"One of the maids was a spy. The cardinal's men came here and kidnapped Lise right out of our yard," said Katje. She looked fire into my eyes. "Christian and Peter escaped."

"I know, they came to the see. They woke Jan first. I couldn't catch him. Did he come here?"

"I was awake." She spoke, shafts of fire blazing from her eyes, only occasionally focusing on me. I think she was making the story clear to herself. "A crowd gathered opposite our gate late last night. I sent to friends at the French embassy, and received word that we might expect a platoon here by morning. They are Father's friends, really. I feared something, and it happened before dawn. I was watching. The crowd is the cardinal's crowd. I knew that by their jeering last night. While it was still dark, I heard a horse galloping down the road. No soldiers had arrived to protect us, and I had just a few men posted inside the gate. I went to the window and watched what I already knew would happen. Armed men emerged from the crowd. Jan rode up to our gate then. Our own people threw it open, as I'd ordered, but it was too late. He killed a cardinal's man before they got him off his horse, but there were so many of them. They carried him away in a bag, Steen, in a sack."

"Seekt." I can still hear my voice as I asked this. What a child I was last year. "Seekt, is Jan all right?"

Seekt was a dark shape outlined in the silver-yellow morning light. The shape sat down heavily.

"Father says he sent enough money to the jail that we can be sure Jan and Lise will be taken care of. Don't worry yet. He says the cardinal wants to try Jan, a big trial."

"Murder?" I asked, but no sound came out other than breath. "For killing?"

"Father says that won't come up. They were only thugs in an ambush."

"What's the trial for?" I said to her.

Her eyes turned to mine with a sympathy I will not ever forget. "For corrupting you."

CHAPTER FIVE

IN THEIR MORNING ROOM, Seekt and Katje tried to discuss specifics with me. Katje would correspond with a great barrister in France; things would be done. But I could not hear anything; I felt underwater, and they were standing above me. I got up from my chair and went to Katje, interrupting her fervent explanation, to hug her. Then I was on my way home.

Only the morning before, I had roused the kitchen staff with my antics, and this morning when I burst in on them they froze. As they stood like stone, I asked, "Has my brother had his coffee yet?" They answered no, and I said I would take it up to him. As I carried the small tray up the staircase I did not rehearse anything to say, any likely approach. I simply felt over the urgency within me and let it harden and grow cold. I became aware, as I climbed, that my twin was asleep at that moment.

I was quiet as I entered his room, not nervous or rushed. How strange it is having a twin. I had to pause to wonder if my own hair bunched up like that when I slept; if my mouth, too, lay partly open, in the shape of an archer's bow; if I, too, ever got that little wrinkle across my chin when the pillow pressed it. I put his coffee on the table by the bed, and sat down gently next to him, gliding onto the sheets, letting my full weight sink only after his eyes fluttered. By that time in my life I felt like an expert at waking people. "Moenen," I said, stroking him. He woke right away, and looked into my eyes as if he'd been awake for a long time.

"Hello," he said. He didn't move.

"I brought you your coffee," I said. Sitting up, he stirred the coffee. My fury was a diamond egg inside me, something perfectly my own, an instrument upon which I could play. I trusted it to be there now. "How did you sleep?" I asked Moenen.

"Fine," he said.

"Moenen, I have a problem."

"I know," he replied.

"How do you know?" My fury began to move toward him.

"Because," Moenen said, "last night I dreamed you were running through a field of wheat, slashing through it with a sword; wheat was flying everywhere. Blackbirds gathered around you thick as rain in the air. Suddenly, we were sitting in front of a fireplace with a big blaze going, sitting in opposite chairs, looking at each other. I was singing to us. You stood up, holding a log or something over your head as if to crush the fire. Then I feared you would crush me, and I heard the blackbirds crying again. I woke up frightened. I thought, Steen is angry about something. Are you?"

"Moenen, they have arrested my friend Jan." For only an instant, something involuntary crossed his face, a brief expansion about the eyes, as if he'd been punched in the chest. But it was gone too quickly for me to be sure. I remember it now only because I didn't believe it then. Moenen gripped the sheet of the bed in his right fist while he leaned over to put his coffee on the table. When he had relaxed back into the bed, I saw that he still gripped the sheet that way, knotting, pulling the folds of linen in his hand. In all that was to come, I wish I could have remembered this one, childlike emblem of his tense hand, Moenen holding on for dear life. I never knew, then, how Moenen had been compromised; I didn't know how Moenen loved what I loved, alone, remote, and solitary as he was.

"Are you upset?" he asked.

I had to suppress urgency and ignore the question. "What can you do to help?"

Here he made a smile so ironic that he looked as if he were twice his age; cynical, as an old man is cynical.

"Steen, I could resign from the council. I mean, that is all I *could* do, normally. That's all I could do. But I can't even do that." And he laughed a lost laugh.

"Can't you influence them, make them let Jan go?"

"No."

"You can't resign then? Aren't you compromised, insulted, that they would pry into the family like this?"

"Yes, but I can't show that. We'll all pretend I didn't know this person, that I don't know of his arrest."

"Why, Moenen? Why?"

"Steen, I can't be anywhere but on their side. Something terrible has happened. My fault. That's why I'm on the council to begin with. I wouldn't have chosen to sit on their court and be a judge, I tell you. But I have to. I can't talk about it. Don't try to make me."

"So I have to fight this by myself?"

"Fight?"

"Yes," I almost screamed. "Get Jan out of jail."

"You can't fight, Steen. They do what they want."

"And if it is tried, you will be one of the judges?" Like a man falling asleep in church, he looked far into the corner of the room.

"Moenen!" I threw myself on him, pounding his shoulders, hitting him hard. "Moenen, stop it. Stop it!" Then I was lying hard against him, pressing his chest, saying *Please* over and over again. He was crying helplessly, looking at the ceiling. He pushed me roughly off the side of the bed.

Between heaves of his chest, between sobs and long gulping breaths, came the resigned, bleak words. "I can't."

I fell toward the doorway, hardly pausing. I remember saying hatefully, "You stink," before I slammed the door.

Katje was at the Hall of Lawyers when I found her that afternoon. I had ridden in our carriage, speeding recklessly through the streets on my rounds, showing the solid coach, slowing before the cardinal's residence, although I avoided the vicinity of the courts building that day. I imagined a bigger display there someday soon. Eventually, I paused to search the lawyers' barracks, where most of them met and dined together. Katje was in the foyer of the dining hall, talking to Governor Iselin, whose party Jan had attended one spring. He was enormous. His wig looked like a tinsel tree atop the dome of a church. They spoke, their heads together, while banqueting noises emanated from the hall inside. I knew that Katje was only slightly acquainted with him, so their intimacy was the more impressive, encouraging to me. She looked very grave, but I knew what even her smallest smile would do to him. His face was that of a leader, sharp and firm, sapient but not tired. While she spoke, he looked over Katje's head with the absent intensity of a doctor taking a pulse. The governor is wonderful. When he saw me, he said my name right away.

"Steen! Why don't we see *you* occasionally at the company? You know—and this will add fuel to the fire Fraulein Seekt has been telling me about—a certain interest in town, a scarlet sort of interest, Steen, has been trying schemes for assuming a vacant seat with us. That is why I want to see one of you Leuwens there more often, keeping your place."

He was right. It made me furious. "I will be at the next sitting, sir. Thank you."

"You are welcome." In his whole manner to me, I noted that Katje must be pleading our cause very well.

"Katje, may I wait for you?" I asked, and she nodded. I wanted to ride her home, or simply ride with her a while and find out what she had been doing for us. Outside, I did not send her coach away; it remained moored alongside ours, rocked by the spirited, smelly, superb horses. Tackle clanked. While I waited there, Young Peter walked around the corner, wearing an enormous and ridiculous hat. Underneath it, he was a shadow. When I hissed, "Peter!" he recognized me; and so the thing under the hat entered the courtyard and walked to my side. "What are you doing here?" I said, drawing him close.

"I just got here from the see. I'm bored. I'm bored with Christian."

"Is he still in the country?"

"Yes."

"You must go back there for now, Peter."

"Soon," he said to me. "Seekt's messenger told us about Jan."

"Peter, you can't make trouble now."

"I know," the darkness under the hat spoke, "the Fredericks said no trouble until Jan is free. But I have an errand. Then I go back, if I can. Our patrols have only one safe road to the city now, did you know that? Did you run into a blockade?"

"Why are you bored with Christian?" I countered.

"He clings to me," Peter said.

"What's wrong with that?" I said. There was a pause. Warm wind blew the big brim of his hat down into his face. "You're not going to your father's, are you?" I asked.

"I'll see you in the country." He turned and made for the street.

"Don't get caught!" I called after him, watching him step over the cobblestones. I stood musing, then, until Katje caught me by the sleeve.

"Is Iselin on our side?" I asked immediately.

"Sort of. It's not that simple."

"Katje." We looked at each other earnestly through the wind. "We could talk," I said. "Couldn't we make some plans now?" She hugged me.

"Send your coach home," she said.

"I thought we'd send yours."

"Nooo . . ." she said.

As we talked, riding in her carriage, Katje looked to me like she was putting forth her every effort. I was not even a little nervous. She spoke and smiled as if she'd vowed to charm the sprites out of the air. What a fortunate girl, so beautiful. It was a privilege to be with her.

"I have a secret," I said.

"What?" She perched her face near mine in perfect anticipation, and I wanted to laugh.

"Peter came through town today. I saw him just now."

Katje leaned back in her seat. We were managing conspirators, the noble and the spy, to each other. "Why is he here?" Katje asked.

"I don't know," I said. "With his temper, he's like a firecracker. I hope he doesn't go for his father."

"Not yet." A flag, a feather of her hair, bright in the sun, blew against the soft black leather upholstery. It was going to be *our* spring.

"Where are we going?" I finally asked. I truly did not care, that afternoon with her, but I asked anyway.

"To a friend of my father's," was all she would say. She told me that she had already sent letters to France by courier. By a stratagem quite illegal and therefore uncertain, she was arranging to have her father empowered as a special embassy of the king at Versailles, so that an inconspicuous guard of French dragoons could be at Seekt's disposal. "Only for extreme cases," Katje said. With Iselin's approval, she would write to request the presence of a famous French clerical lawyer. He would attend, as an observer, whatever proceedings there might be. It would draw Europe's attention to our case, and perhaps make our judges behave less barbarously. Iselin, besides approving this maneuver, had advised that Jan have a reputable lawyer, a man who would be a good representative among our peers.

"Could we isolate the burghers and the cardinal and turn people against them?" I ventured.

By way of an answer, Katje's eyes lit up only a little.

The canals grow narrower, and brackish, and there began to appear unused tracts of marshland. I dimly remembered coming this way with my father once, to visit a business of ours where they made fishnets in a barn. At the entrance to the barn, an old, old man had kissed my father's hand, then asked me if they fed me to make me big. He said he was Italian, from Roma, and he asked me, bending down, if they fed me spaghetti to make me big. I remember I said no, but I had eaten macaroni. He laughed at me, or with me. I remember my father was kind to him. When my father was talking business inside, I ran back out to our carriage, where Moenen had stayed. He was still huddled in his corner of the seat. There was a streak of silver-gold sunlight across the top of his head. He grabbed me and held on to me as if I were his own self, or his soul, that he was trying to cling to. The sun dimmed; clouds were racing over the sky. We played spy or something until our father returned.

That memory faded as Katje's carriage took us onto a road I'd never been on before, a long track of packed yellow sand that led across the waste of marshland. From the window it looked as if we were riding on air above the reeds and mud. Seabirds rose in lazy, hesitant circles over little pools among the grasses. I was exhausted; I began to feel sad and desperate again as I gazed at the marshes. I had a fantasy, imagining that someone came to tell me that my wife Katje had just given birth to our first son, and all I did in response was to raise my eyebrows in a worldly, sour look, and go on drinking. I would be looking over the world from some high balcony; I think it was Seekt's observatory where I imagined that little scene taking place.

Katje was silent, too. We both gazed, abstracted, from the carriage windows. And then we jumped as a loud crack burst through the air. It sounded like a cannon. The vista from my window came to life as hundreds, maybe thousands of birds rose over the endless marsh, their ragged cries cued by the shot. To the far horizon the air was filled with their panicked shapes. Their screams, which startled me more than the cannon had, sounded like a family quarrel on the stairs of hell.

I turned from the unpleasant noise and said, "Where are we *going?*"

"We are *going,*" she replied, turning to me with a fresh breeze on things, "to get a letter of mark. Do you know what that is? It is an old-fashioned but still legal way of getting around rules. Such a letter can be given only by royalty. My father got us an appointment with an old friend of his. Have you ever heard of the Prins Nassau?"

She explained that we were bound for the isolated seaside palace of a cousin of our former rulers, William and Mary, who went to reign in England. This Prins Nassau was a relic of another generation. A famous eccentric, he was on close terms with many European monarchs. He never married, and he had long since retired to spend his sixth and then his seventh decades alone on his estate. He was a prince of enormous wealth and, because he was a royal prince, his word was still law in the Netherlands.

It must have been his cannon we'd heard. The avenue became wider as poplar trees appeared on either side, masking the hideous horizon, then soon we emerged into a fortresslike courtyard. On the seaward side, three stories above the ground, a row of cannons pointed through embrasures. A guard in a crisp blue uniform paced back and forth. A footman in the same blue met our carriage, running down to us from the side of the double bow stairway. He led us back up the staircase. Katje gave him a letter from Seekt, and we were shown inside. The letter was handed to another, younger footman, who led us down the longest corridor I had ever seen in my life. There must have been twenty doors leading off either side. It was gloomy, because there were only occasional windows which showed little courtyards inside the palace as we moved along. At the end were double doors as high as heaven. The footman closed them behind him, so we knew we were waiting outside the prince's room. The sounds of a harpsichord came to us, a booming, brutal bass in the left hand, and a tinkling melody in the right, plucked out in nervous triplets. It was, I recognized, the half-sane music of Scarlatti. The echoes sounded like cannonballs careening down a glacier. Eventually the music stopped, and we heard the machinery of the giant latch as both doors swung wide into the room, the footman bending to us in a graceful bow. A strange noise, another strange noise, accompanied the parting of the doors.

It was the sound of leaves on a terrace in autumn, scraping along the ground, crackling as they were brushed back under the doors. Our eyes widened as we walked into the long room, and our feet crushed small piles, drifts of dead leaves by the entrance. It was a vast ballroom, high-ceilinged, in ornate white plaster and gilding. Mythological pastorals were painted on the arched ceiling in pastels. Light came into the room from a row of glass double doors, as in my gallery at home, only these were much taller. Squares of miniature trees outside, and some big shade trees, were the source of the dead leaves. Eddies of leaves skittered, circling across the gleaming parquet.

Katje and I did not glance at each other. The presence of royalty focuses one's attention rather completely. At the far end of the room stood the prins. Down there, a small fire hid under an Olympian mantel, as though inside its own house. The prins's harpsichord stood to one side, and a small writing table and tapestry chair were positioned under yet another pair of huge glass double doors. A glint of gold flickered from the desk—an inkwell or a pen, I supposed.

His frock coat and knee breeches were of gray velvet.

There was one gold decoration on his breast. As we proceeded toward him his figure grew larger. I could see that the velvet he wore was of a gray that somehow implied rest and silence. I have never again seen such white, white silk as his shirt and hose were made of. Twenty paces from him Katje stopped us and we bowed. A gust of spring air under one of the doors scattered leaves behind us. In a sunbeam, the prins's head shone like the polished floor. He was utterly bald.

"I received your message. How kind of you to visit me," he said, motioning us toward nearby chairs. I noticed a leather folding stool standing by his harpsichord at an abandoned angle. I was certain it was he who had been playing; I imagined one of the strings still resonating, humming inside the inlaid box. Leaning against a chair opposite us, the prins asked Katje, "Is your papa still as fat as a goose?" and she giggled in spite of herself, tossing her hair. It was wonderful to see her having an involuntary reaction. Then he looked me up and down, in a way I had never been looked at before. Like a tailor appraising a bolt of cloth, and no apology in the look despite its boldness. Yet it made me feel good.

His face was a cascade of wrinkles, but two things gave him an eerie childishness. His eyes were bright, and as catchable, it seemed, as a little child's eyes; and his lips were large, perfectly red and moist. Perhaps some arts of the makeup table had been employed there, but I think not. They were simply unusually large and robust red lips. Such full lips in that withered face were unsettling. Perhaps he knew so.

"Your father was a good horseman and a loyal knight," he said, ending his inspection directly in my eyes. "Do you know how very well he rode a horse? We were sorry to lose him." As he said this to me, with a special intimacy that seemed a gift, I began to feel comfortable. I belonged in that room, somehow. I noticed then that the air was different from any air I had ever smelled, an intriguing odor, faintly sweet, definitely achieved. He stood with the light behind him, his still form outlined in a halo when the intermittent April sun came out again. Suddenly, as if he were not visible when he moved, the prins was beside me,

MY BROTHER'S IMAGE

bending to whisper near my ear. There was his skull, cool near my ear, and the breath tickling.

"Peter is here," said the prins.

My eyebrows shot upward and my vision locked on the slim orange tree outside the window.

He propped my head with a careless motion and looked across at Katje, his wrinkled face side by side with mine. He said to her, ". . . and a beehive has dropped on you both. I must help you." As he abandoned his whispering position he straightened his posture and moved behind me, still addressing Katje. "So, mademoiselle, you young people will take on the burghers now, hm?" *That's* where I learned the term "burgher." He crossed to her, slowly, like a connoisseur approaching a painting. "Surely your papa," he said—meaning a different "papa"—"the king of France, will give you in marriage when you marry your viscomte." Katje grinned in her eyes as he bent to her.

"Will you and my father fix it?" she asked, laughing up, laughing, I think, at life.

"It is you who has fixed it, mademoiselle, and your father humbly here behind the scenes. He is proud of you." I caught his whispered, "and of your intelligence." She dipped her head to him.

He sat down, the emblem flashing on his chest, one leg forward of the other, arms flat on the armrests. "Shall I give you a letter of mark, mademoiselle?"

"I think it should be for Steen, sir," Katje said to him.

"As you wish." Gliding to his writing desk, he said to me, "I need to know your destination. To assure the passage of the person named in the letter, a captain of mine will deliver this one half-hour before you arrive. He will wait to see that you are treated properly. Where is it you wish to visit, Steen?"

"The prison," I said.

Katje went to his desk and said, "Is there any hope of intervention, sir?"

"Not yet, not yet," he soothed. He turned to a set of ten little gold bells lined up on the desk in graduated sizes. That was what had sparkled. He rang the sixth largest bell. Katje sat again, while the prins took up a pen and began to scratch in ink on a square of parchment. A footman entered from a door by the mantel, carrying a tray. The prins sprinkled sand on his writing and the footman placed before him a brazier that burned under a tiny crucible of wax. He handed the prins a pestle, his seal. Blue wax was poured onto the parchment, and the prins impressed his seal. Then he whispered in the footman's ear and the man took away the tray.

With his hand resting on the desk, the prins turned to me and said, "Now the minion kneels." I went to him and knelt.

"Promise me you will behave sensibly, Steen. This commission from our house puts you above the law. Will you be responsible with it?"

"I will," I said, looking up at his form in the light.

"Your father was a careful man. He never overstepped his bounds."

"I promise."

"I want you to discuss all your plans with Seekt, beforehand. Tell him on what day and hour you want to make your first visit to your friend, and this letter will precede you. After that, my captain will be at Seekt's service, and will keep the letter in his care for you."

Katje watched me as I rose and sat down again.

"Now I have a surprise for you both," said the prins. The door by the mantel opened again. "First, Steen, this is your captain, Captain van der See. Captain, this is the letter of mark. Herr van Seekt will send for you when it is needed. That is young Herr van Leuwen, in whose service you will be." The captain put the letter into a leather case he was carrying. As he left the room, he stopped before my chair, clicked his heels, and bowed sharply.

"Now the surprise," said the prins, and Peter walked into the room through the high French doors. He did not look at us, but went straight to the Prins Nassau, bowed, then looked down at the old man, who was inches less tall than Peter had become. "Have you finished practicing?" Peter said.

The prins took Peter's arms and turned him to face us. As he recognized us his face lit up and he blushed.

"Peter has been my occasional guest here since the day when I caught him stealing an apple from my garden. This was his punishment, to be my occasional guest. Say hello to your friends, Peter."

Peter walked to us, smiled, and hugged Katje. He was embarrassed. When he hugged me, he whispered, "Don't tell Christian. Promise?" I promised.

Peter was very quiet. I was embarrassed for him. The prins simply watched him, then Peter turned and said, "I tested it."

"Yes, I heard the shot. Did they show you how it is operated?"

Peter nodded.

"Are you sure? I don't want an accident. I don't want you hurt, Peter."

"I can operate it, and I can teach someone to help me. I worked with it for almost an hour." He faced me, and his eyes were very formal. "I'm taking a cannon to the see," he explained. "The prins has given me a cannon, and his troops will go with me so we can get through the barricades. Did you hear my test shot?"

I nodded, trying with my eyes to make him smile, but it didn't work. He said to the prins, "May we go now? It's mounted for traveling."

"Yes," said the prins, "be gone—and stay out of trouble. I will see you next week."

Peter ran from the room, a loping, but graceful, run.

I approached one of the glass doors in time to see Peter astride his cannon, riding among four of the prins's blue-uniformed soldiers. Peter looked radiant, riding backward on his cannon down the sandy road under the poplars, into shadow. When I turned back to the room Katje was standing alone in front of the mantel. She watched me as I walked out of the light; that was the first time I remember her watching me carefully, fully, like that. Her eyes told me that the prins had left us alone. I wouldn't see him again that day. She looked so serious— black dress, blond hair. I reveled in it. It was like bathing in a dreamed-of fountain. I was so tired, so impressed by then, that I felt intense, already nostalgic for the moment at hand.

"We're going to win!" I said to Katje, and our embrace was better, sexier, because it was not executed, only imagined. We embraced in ghost fashion, while yearning to embrace. "We're going to win," I said, the yearning still there.

"No intervention," Katje said, shaking her head at me.

"So?"

"It's not the best," she said.

"But I have my writ. You have the lawyers. And Peter is taking a cannon to the see!" I took her by the shoulders, and it was so delicious to hold her, for whatever ostensible reason. She laughed ruefully.

"Oh, that cannon," Katje said over my shoulder, "that is the prins playing with Peter. Get me out of here." She held on to me, but still she was the one leading as we marched down the length of the ballroom. Katje kicked hard at a drift of dry leaves.

In the hall, while the footman went for our coach, she hung on me, clung, rocking back and forth. That was when I became frightened. For the first time since my dawn ride, I realized that something might go wrong about Jan. As we rode home I kept imagining Peter riding away on the prins's cannon, the cannon passing triumphantly through military barricades. Still, fear stayed in my muscles.

Because we were confidantes, I could reach across the seat to Katje and, while she stared through her window, run my finger down the line of blond hair along the side of her face. I smoothed her hair at the back. She turned to me very quickly all of a sudden and said, "You don't know anything, do you?"

I put my head down. "I know what to do," I muttered.

She grabbed me, dragging me over to her side so that my head was lying in her lap. *She* was stroking *my* hair, and then her hands ran over and over my face, feeling the features of it like a blind person. I kept my eyes closed.

"It will be all right, won't it?" I said, but before I had finished she was running her fingers along my lips, then along the front of my teeth, passing her fingers across my teeth and lips. She said, "Steen, Steen." With her hand at my mouth that way, I couldn't think about anything but the two of us, about me. I got an erection. She didn't stop. My heart was going very fast. I had never touched a woman's breasts. I didn't know how they worked. I had never seen between a woman's legs. Did you have to be very careful there? Could you hurt something? How did it please her? What if you didn't know what you were doing?.

Pretty soon, with her hand on my face, I began to daydream, to doze, and I went to sleep for a while. I was dreaming of a cool night, Jan coming down a rope against the rough prison wall, landing in front of me, his erection pressing against my stomach as he lifted me off my feet to kiss me, our mouths open. "Do you want to do it with Katje?" he chuckled at me. "Little flower, do you want to know how?"

The carriage stopped. It was getting to be dusk. Outside the window I saw Seekt's carriage yard. Katje's head loomed over me, her long hair falling on my face. I blinked, waking as she leaned over me.

"Everything is going to move very fast now, all right?" Katje said. I could only look at her. "Be yourself. You are very beautiful," she was saying. "You will have to do what you feel, Steen. Stand up for yourself." She stroked my hair some more. "We're going to do everything we can, but we don't know what will happen. You . . . find your desires and do them. And when you think back on this you'll be proud. You'll know everything. All right?" Because I was still tired, one tear, just one, broke from my right eye and rolled down into my ear. She dried its track softly with her hand. Still lying across her lap, I reached over my head and found the door handle, all the while looking into her eyes. I flung the carriage door open and, wordless, we got out.

We stood for a minute in front of Seekt's carved oak door, a warm spring breeze on us, the pink sunset around the corner of the house. What was romantic was that we stood side by side for a moment, steeling ourselves, breathing deeply together without looking at each other. Strangely, strangely, a dry leaf scraped across the terrace between the door and us. We looked at each other. "Strange," my eyes implied, and we moved to the door together.

We took off our cloaks and presented ourselves in the dining room at the foot of Seekt's long table. He was sitting at the head of it, alone, gazing at us. His fat features, his white moustache, were benign. There was a great but somehow impotent kindness in his eyes. He said, "Crusaders need good meals, children." He spread his arms wide, indicating the two chairs nearest him. We sat, and began to eat shellfish.

"We got the letter," I told him. "In my name. Can I visit Jan tonight?"

"No. Tomorrow night. Tomorrow," said Seekt, "I will send word to the captain to wait for you there. I also want one of our lawyers to go with you. Now, Steen, the trial is set for only four days from today. Tomorrow morning we are going to have a conference and make our plans. I have feelers out among the court, and tomorrow we may know more about what kind of case they'll make. Until our conference tomorrow, let us not make any plans."

"Except that I shall visit Jan tomorrow."

"Yes, that's certain," he said. "Also, I have arranged for Lise's release. She will be back with us before the trial. They don't really want her, you see."

I told Seekt about Peter and the cannon, about which I was still exuberant. Seekt looked worried. "This must stop," he muttered, Katje looking at him, "this must stop." Just after the meat course, Seekt rose slowly from his chair and said good-night to us. He padded out of the room, more an old man than I had ever seen him.

"Watch, Katje," I said, breaking the silence after the door had closed behind her father. "Watch." She looked across at me.

"Is this going to be some gross table trick?" she asked, such real moroseness in her voice that I said flippantly, "You mean, am I going to stick out my tongue with food all over it?" I laid my almost empty wineglass on its side. There was still enough wine in it to make it appear that the wine would run out onto the cloth, but the glass was curved, so it held the wine within itself, rolling in a circle when I set it in motion. "See? Have you already seen that?"

She looked at me, head to one side. Then she rose and came around the table. She put her hand in mine and we walked out of the room. We walked all around the house and through the gardens in the dark. There were tulip buds and rosebuds and lilac; the grass was wet. We went to the stables after a time and climbed the narrow stairs. Katje led us down the gallery to one of the beds. She lit a candle. I hugged her to me very hard.

It was all fun, and I let her show me what was what.

CHAPTER SIX

WHEN I ENTERED Seekt's house the next morning for our meeting with the lawyers, Katje saw me in the hall. She became almost formal, straightening her body and taking my hand as she led me to Seekt's library. Frederick One was there, sitting by Seekt, and on Seekt's other side were two gentlemen I guessed were lawyers. Katje and I took chairs. One of the lawyers spoke first.

"He will be charged as a corrupter of the young and as an immoral influence in society. I am also told that if he does not confess to those charges he is liable to be taken outside and burned at the stake."

Seekt said, "Will they call witnesses?"

"No," was the reply, "but the official charge contains some reference about one of the city's first families. They are assuming that he will plead guilty sooner if he can hope to keep our young friend's name out of it. They hope for a quick confession after the reading of the charge. They are now working on him. 'Pleading with him,' they call it."

"Do you mean he is being tortured?" I asked, standing up.

"Young sir, they are not known to be gentle," he replied.

"Herr Seekt, I want to go there now," I said. Katje drew me back into my chair.

"Tonight, Steen," Seekt said, not gruffly, but definitely. Frederick One caught my eye and signaled that he wanted to see me outside.

Gliding a careful eye over me every few seconds, Seekt went on, "How then, can the case be disputed, if no specifics are named? No one can come to his defense if no one is named."

"Exactly," answered the second lawyer. "No one can defend him, or themselves, against a general indictment. On the one hand they disarm his friends, and on the other they make him capitulate so he will not have to implicate anyone who could help him. It is ingenious."

"Can we not sue for his release?" asked Katje.

"Who is 'we'?" asked the second lawyer, a large man, without opening his eyes.

"A group of interested citizens."

"No," the first lawyer said smoothly. We waited, silent. "Not without first petitioning the court for recognition as involved citizens. And their position is that they are not hearing petitions because this is a special court."

"Can't the Prins Nassau help us?" I burst out. The two lawyers looked at each other.

"He could, I think," said the first lawyer after a moment. "A representative of his could become involved, yes."

Seekt said, "Yes, that is a recourse and it sounds like it is the only one we can plan to use. Do you gentlemen know of any other way to be heard by the court?"

The lawyers shook their heads.

Frederick met me outside the library and we leaned against the wall together.

"Will you use your writ and visit Jan tonight?" Frederick asked. I nodded. "When you visit, keep your eyes very wide open. Be alert to everything about how the prison is run. See how we might get Jan out."

"Yes. I see," I said.

"Notice how the guards are stationed. See if there are any doors or windows left open anywhere. See if any of the guards seem drunk. In fact, let's give you a flask—a couple of flasks—of strong stuff. Give them to the guards."

"Silver flasks, so they won't refuse," I suggested.

"Sweet boy," said Frederick.

"We'll have to hope they save some for tomorrow night, because that will be our first chance to rescue him," I said.

"No, it isn't. What's wrong with tonight?" asked Frederick. "As soon as you return with the information, we can go back and get him."

"We meet tonight, then," I said, "here, in the quarters

over the stables. Bring some people in from the country and wait for me. I'll come as soon as I leave Jan."

"All right."

"Promise?" I said.

"Of course."

Then I ran back in to Seekt, asking when I could visit the prins to try again to get help with the court. I found Katje asking him the same thing.

"But I had better not go, because he demurred once already when I asked him," she said.

"Steen and I can go. That's a good combination," said Seekt, "but I will first have to get permission to visit, as I got permission for you. I will send a messenger. It is unlikely he will see us this afternoon, and tonight Steen will be at the jail. We can hope to see the prins tomorrow."

That made me impatient, but I knew better than to press it. Katje's eyes told me it had to be so. So she and I then walked into the delightful bright morning; late April tulips on Seekt's lawn. Katje stopped and stared at the ground, then up at the sky. "I like you, Steen. I like you," she said to the sky.

I thought back to only a few months before; when I was a little virgin admiring her, coveting her acquaintance, as we ate our dinner on my mother's stairs. I thought, Life has given me what I wanted without taking anything in return.

Katje and I said good-bye to Frederick as he mounted to ride to the see. He was a strong rider, and he threw his fine legs astride the horse with masterful ease. His hips seemed to merge into the back of the horse as he sat there. Then the horse grew fractious, and the image of the centaur grew more vivid as they plunged, he seeming to control the animal from his hips. The horse bounced them around in a circle, and Frederick kept his stare on us. Finally, as he came around again, he leaned down and kissed Katje's upraised hand. Then he rode off.

The first casualty came home that afternoon. Lise arrived from jail. She had no news about Jan. She had been kept completely alone, and the first official who spoke to her at all was the guard who told her she was free. Poor Lise; she was panicky and haggard. Her beauty did not bear adversity well. She cried in Katje's arms the moment she fell from Seekt's carriage. I became annoyed with her when she couldn't answer any of my questions about the jail. Bewildered, without perspective, she seemed an unintelligent girl, but then I thought of the hell she had been through. I was sorry I had been so quick to judge her. Katje led her inside and I wandered in the garden.

Wandering, I had an experience that haunts me still. I was worrying about Jan's escape, and dreaming about whether I might be sleeping with him that very night. I was frightened about the prison; was he in misery, and I impotent to help? What would happen to the feelings with him that I had come to count on as a sort of daily bread? Flowers and grass and sky minded not.

Fighting that feeling inside me was the natural feeling of the growth of things, the sovereignty of the sap in the veins of April, the rule of newness. But then the shadow returned; Jan was in chains. I walked near a fence with fields stretching beyond it. There was a figure on the other side of the fence. He had been watching me. You can tell, you can feel another person's attention if you admit you can. He was some distance away, down the lawn and over the fence; but because of his having been watching me, and my knowing it, the bond between us was palpable. I examined him; a young man, fair enough, exuding a certain sensuous air. Perhaps that came from the intensity of his gaze when he turned it on me again. Watching him, I saw there was a bulge in his pants. I half saw it, half just knew it was there. The chemistry of such encounters does not diminish beyond the confines of a bedroom. So I was momentarily, mechanically, also interested, and I felt my own quick heat. As I walked closer, he looked toward a clump of bushes nearby, and then walked that way, glancing over his shoulder occasionally.

I was about to follow him when I realized that all my thoughts had flown out of my head. I was like an animal going to water. Not so bad in itself, perhaps, but I had a beautiful friend to consider, and what would be accomplished in the bushes? A vision rose to me, and I saw hundreds of such encounters, hiding endlessly in little places throughout my future. I was afraid. I ran—actually ran—back to a place in Seekt's garden where I could not be seen. I sat there to collect myself, breathing quite hard. Would it always excite me? How often would I follow?

As I sat in that garden, it became increasingly horrible to think of a world without Jan in it. The feeling was so urgent that I ran to Seekt in the house to see if the prins had granted us an appointment. Seekt had not even sent the messenger yet. Meanwhile, Captain van der See would meet me at the jail at eight o'clock that night; we might have heard from the prins by the time I returned. I drifted into the library, waiting for dinner. I could not read. Not with any intelligence, though I tried.

They came to tell me that it was time for dinner. Too nervous to eat, I said to give Herr Seekt my compliments and to tell him I would see him after dinner. The evening was surprisingly warm, so I wandered in the garden a while. My rambles took me toward the stables, and naturally I found the door to the upstairs again. I climbed the small circular stair and entered the room at the top. The chandeliers hung up there in the dusk, and the long dining table, stained from a thousand dinners, stretched into a dark corner, its wine marks and grease spots barely visible, like ghost ponds in a marsh. I lit a candle and paced the length of the gallery. After a time, I stood. My eyes became unfocused; I drifted into a buzzing, semi-waking state, swaying where I stood. You know that high-pitched note in your ear when there is total silence?

Eventually I came awake and took up my candle again. It had grown to full dark, and I knew that soon I should go and talk to Seekt before setting off for the jail. But first I had one more stop to make. I wanted to see Jan's studio, to feel again our first encounter there. I walked to the end of the gallery where the door to the studio was. Approaching it, I paused by the bed where Katje and I had lain. I thought I saw Jan's figure leaning in the doorframe the way he had when he'd said good-bye to me that first afternoon. I was frightened at first, before I recognized what that shadow was, a memory. I took a deep breath and pushed at the door. My candle guttered as it swung open. Then the room leaped to light in front of me. A gaunt easel stood empty in the center, like a skeleton of his work. There was the smell of linseed oil and the pollens of spring in the cool air. Through the window in the roof, stars twinkled. I leaned against the wall. As soon as I did, I collapsed inwardly, tired, wanting to cry. I breathed deeply for a while, looking up at the stars until I got my equilibrium back. Then I saw it: the flickering light from my candle was catching a rich tint on the wall behind the easel. I found my balance again, and carried my candle over to the wall. There, hanging on a nail, was the gold watch the parson had given Jan. One thing he'd forgotten in his flight to the country. Or maybe, I thought, something he'd left behind to keep his place, for luck. I lifted it off the nail and put it in my pocket. Then I walked back, slowly, through the gallery, savoring it, savoring the fact that I'd left the door to his studio open, savoring the treasure-chest sweetness of the spring air in that year of my life.

Seekt was waiting for me in the library, dozing in his huge chair. He tried to be jovial when I bumbled in, but I could see the sleep still misting his old head and his eyes. He told me that the prins would see us the next afternoon at three o'clock. This relieved me a little. Then we discussed my visit to the jail.

"You will be met by Captain van der See at the office of the overseer, within the walls. To get inside, just say your name; you are expected. Lawyer van Patten will meet you there as well, inside."

"Is that the sleepy one?" I asked, immediately embarrassed because of Seekt's own groggy state.

But Seekt was a kind man. "Like me tonight, full of years and nodding? Yes, that would describe him, but only on the surface. In fact, that manner of his is more than a little cultivated. Beneath it he has great acumen. And power. Wait till you see him in action. He is a very good man to have by us now."

"I should go now."

Seekt nodded.

"I will need to stop at home on my way there, so that will require a few extra minutes."

"Steen, remember that we are most anxious that nothing untoward should happen during your visit. No illegalities, no little knives or other attempts that would reflect on the prins. The prins must not be alienated from us. We will need all the help we can get in court the day after tomorrow. And remember that we see the prins tomorrow to ask him to intercede. Since that may be our only help, it is vital that you do nothing to compromise us tonight. Do you understand?"

I nodded.

"My coach is waiting for you," he said. As he was proposing to tell me someday about the lady from whom he got the coach, I ran and hugged him. His eyes were moist. "Take care, *soit sage,* Steen." I ran out to the carriage. Matt was up on the box, barely visible in the dark.

"To my house first," I shouted, and when he heard me bang the door closed, we were off.

Do you know that sensation of no time passing? It seemed we'd arrived at my own front door before I had even left Seekt's; the journey had been swallowed by the night. It seemed I hadn't been home in years, not merely two days since I'd slept alone. I raced through the hall. Light from the dining room meant that mother was entertaining. Somehow, I knew that Moenen was not in the house. I went to my father's silver collection in the library.

My hand paused above two silver flasks for the jailers, a matched set with our crest on them. The candles were lighted in the library, so I knew the guests would come there and I would have to be gone soon. My head whirled. I was terrified about going against the prins, against Seekt's wishes, against my word. Would an escape attempt turn the prins against us? Could we get Jan out legally? Then I thought, But no escape is certain either; that could fail too. One more night before the trial. Deciding to leave the escape plot off for now, I raced out again, back to Seekt's carriage. At least I could reconnoiter the jail that night. I would observe very carefully.

The coach crashed through the streets like a comet. Lighted housefronts sped by, blurring. The coach lurched and jolted, tossing me sideways; it seemed to scrape the

MY BROTHER'S IMAGE 111

road. I saw the walls of the prison. Such big, big stones they built it of; they looked as big as houses.

I heard Matt shout my name, and then an awful screeching of metal on metal, the sound of chains, and in the flickering torches I saw a huge iron portcullis slowly, jerkily lifting off the ground. As we passed under it, I feared the sharp, rusty spikes would crash down and impale the coach, but it hung in the air. As the carriage stopped, I saw lights in one of the windows that gave onto the courtyard, and there was a fine roan horse by that window, with the prins's crest on its blue saddlecloth. So, the captain was waiting. Climbing down, I saw another carriage. Lawyer van Patten's, I thought.

I never expected it, but as Matt arranged himself to wait for me on his box, he called to me, "Good luck, boy." They were the only words he had ever said to me in his life.

The good feeling of that was erased even before I reached the lighted doorstep. From a bigger door on the other side of the courtyard a figure emerged, running. As he passed under one of the torches on the wall I saw that it was Moenen. He stumbled once, as if he couldn't see where he was going. And then I saw tears on his cheek. Quickly he was up on a horse that hid in a shadowed corner, and he rode out under the portcullis. I don't believe he saw me.

As I entered the warden's office I was wondering what Moenen could possibly have been doing in the prison, and why the tears, weeper though he sometimes was. So my entrance was more nonchalant, because of my self-absorption, than I could have made it on purpose.

A little stone room with a wonderfully cozy fireplace, a wooden table—this was clearly the overseer's living quarters. As I came in, van Patten, the captain, and the overseer turned. The overseer was a little wizened man with the air and manner of an unhappy clerk. I think he was intimidated by us. He read the letter of mark, which the captain handed to him, very slowly.

I was glad of van Patten's presence soon enough, when that worthy said to the warden in a masterful tone, "Now, Warden, the young master and I will permit one of your men to guide us to Jan of Soest, painter, whom you have in your care here. As soon as we have returned, this captain will return to His Royal Highness and assure him that his letter of mark was properly honored. I do not expect our visit to inconvenience you, Warden, for more than three-quarters of an hour. Is that clear?"

The overseer nodded meekly and called for one of his men. As the captain bowed and took back the letter from the warden's hands, I took an opportunity: "Have there been other visitors here tonight, Warden?"

It gave him his chance. With an attempt of looking taller, he said, "By law, sir, no visitors are permitted here." I smiled at him. He shrank again. When a guard appeared at the door, he directed the man to take us to Jan's cell.

The journey was horrible. The guard, a dirty, haughty man, seemed to sneer at me every time he showed me his face. Once we turned a corner before lawyer van Patten did, and the man bent to my ear and said, "Come to see your husband?" I dropped back immediately, walking slowly by van Patten's ample side. The corridor opened into a long hall, possibly a dining hall when this place was a castle. A few torches along the walls gave only a little light. It was the most horrible room I have ever seen. Both walls were lined with people, or what had once been people. I think, in most cases, their crime was poverty. Here and there a lunatic was writhing or praying or coughing incessantly, as if trying to tear his throat. The place stank of gin and beer and piss. When a little boy ran from his mother's pallet and clutched my waist, stopping us, the guard turned and sneered at me. The boy was so thin that I wanted to cry. He clutched me, digging his feet into the filthy floor, holding on for dear life. "Want to play? Want to play?" I said I couldn't. I quickly gave him a coin, but before he could pocket it his mother lurched to her feet slurring, "Cornelius, Cornelius." He looked reflexively, with hope, in her direction when he heard his name. But then she came and slapped him so hard that he fell to the floor. She clawed the coin out of his hand. Van Patten hurried me on. I had heard the boy's skull hit the stones.

We were led to a tower with a round area, off which gave a few doorways crossed by iron bars. In the center, at a table, sat an old man. He seemed to have a kindly face until you saw that there was no intelligence, no spark in his eyes; they were watery and blank. He no sooner saw me than he began to caw like a parrot. He did not cease this noise. Looking at me, he began to say words in exact imitation of the way parrots talk. "Pretty boy, want beer? Pretty boy, brandy?" and then the raucous laughter of a parrot. He stopped the awful laugh when van Patten emerged into the light and stamped his cane in front of the man. The guard, our shepherd, was worse than useless, and van Patten had to explain why we had come. The old man's expression was uniformly obscene and he cared nothing for van Patten's authority. He said, "All right, but no lovey-dovey stuff," and again the horrible laughter, which the other guard then joined.

I could not see into the cell. It was too dark. Then two hands appeared, holding the bars, and I knew that it was Jan. I did not run. Because they were watching me, I forced myself to walk normally, steadily, to the hands. I could see only the outline of him in there, but I put my hands over his, shielding this with my body, and said his name, looking into the dark. His fingers intertwined with mine. "May we have light, please," I said over my shoulder, and a torch was brought and placed in a bracket on the slimy stone wall nearby. His face shone in the light. He looked at me patiently. We said nothing at first, just feeling the pressure of our fingers on each other.

Then I saw it, the clotted, deep gashes on his wrists, blood looking as if still wet. And on his neck, welts and bruises. I looked away, vowing not to let him know I'd seen.

Finally he spoke, first looking over my shoulder and then back to me. "Who is that with you, in black? Is that your new lover, hm? Couldn't you wait for me?"

"Jan, that's van Patten, one of the lawyers Seekt has gotten for you. And we have the Prins Nassau; he's going to help us."

"Who?" Jan asked.

"The Prins Nassau. I got here on a letter of his, and he's going to help at your trial. It's going to be all right, Jan, it is."

Jan smiled at me; I pressed his fingers hard.

"Do you get food?" I asked.

He nodded. "Seekt must have bribed someone because I do have decent food. It's been decent, Steen, not too bad—"

"Do you have a window?" I interrupted.

"Yes," he said. "It's tiny and thin, like the spine of a Bible. Why?"

I told him that they wanted to try to rescue him, and he immediately said no, no, whispering it wouldn't be wise, not yet, probably impossible anyway. Then we were cut off by both the guards saying time was up, mocking us, calling to us in falsetto voices. We looked and looked at each other. "You'll be home day after tomorrow," I said as van Patten put his hand on my shoulder.

"Is that when the trial is?" Jan asked, and I felt sorry for him. I hadn't wanted to feel sorry. Yes, I nodded, being led away, looking back at him.

"Oh!" I exclaimed, breaking free and running back to him. Hiding this with my body, pretending it was a last embrace, I palmed his gold watch out of my pocket and into his hand. He looked at me with surprise and admiration when he saw what it was. He caught at me as I turned away, reached through the bars and caught my sleeve, whispering, "But what time is it, what time?"

"I don't know. Ah, maybe eight-thirty," I whispered, looking back. He winked at me, and as he retreated into the darkness I saw his bloodied hands winding the watch.

The two guards stood on either side of the doorway as van Patten and I left the tower. The old jailer said to me, "You look like that other one; I thought you were the same. Two faggots in one day, my my," and then the other guard silenced the man, actually putting a hand over his mouth, saying, "You idiot. Quiet." Moenen had been *here*. Why?

We were moving swiftly now through the damp corridors under low, arched stone vaulting hung with rotting masonry and plaster. The guard kept hurrying us, almost shoving us from behind with his torch. But in the great hall, that horrible place, I stopped. Lying near his mother, the thin little boy slept, curled into a ball, sucking his thumb. I went to him and lifted him into my arms. The mother lunged at me, but I kicked her away and strode out

MY BROTHER'S IMAGE

of the room carrying the boy. "I'm taking you home," I whispered to him.

"Mommy too?" he asked, bleary.

"Maybe later," I said, hurrying. "You first. You'll like it. Lots of food." He hugged me, looking past my shoulder at nothing.

Before the guard could stop me, I was back in the safety of the warden's room, with the captain and van Patten. Immediately, I asked the captain, "Does the prins's authority enable me to save this child from this place?"

The captain looked at the condition of the boy and simply nodded, so that the warden could not miss it. As I walked into the courtyard, the guard, our shepherd, snarled at me, "I bet I know what you want with *him*," and he leered at me. But not for long, because suddenly lawyer van Patten had, with one arm, lifted the man off his feet and into a corner, where he dropped him. He lay, protecting his face with his hand. The captain stepped over him, and then we were in the clean air outside. The captain shouted into the dark: "By order of His Royal Highness, open the gates." Carrying my little bag of bones, Cornelius, I climbed into the carriage. The hideous metal din began again. The captain rode beside our coach's window as we passed under the stone arch and out into the night.

At first, Cornelius couldn't take his eyes off the captain on his horse beside us, but by the time we pulled through Seekt's gate he was sleeping, head on my lap. I carried him straight through the house to the kitchens, where Maria sat by her fire. Seeing his condition, she rose immediately to take him into her arms. I whispered his story to her, then looked down into his face. He was awake, his great empty eyes devoid of expression, terribly passive. I told him Maria would feed him and tell him a story; I said she knew the best stories. He looked at her with intense interest. I left them as Maria set him in a chair and began to prepare a meal. He lolled his head on the back of the chair. I returned for an instant to smooth his hair back and kiss his forehead.

In the library, van Patten was reporting to Seekt. The captain stood looking out into the night. When I entered, the captain returned the letter of mark to Seekt, bowed to us, and went on his way. In the brief silence that followed,

Seekt said, to no one in particular, "My chest hurts." He breathed hard for a bit, then added, "Can't get my breath." Van Patten looked at him quite seriously until Seekt said, "Go on. What more? Is he getting proper food?"

"Yes," I answered quickly, "he thanks you for that. It's been quite decent, he said."

"Now what about this child you've brought home, Steen?"

"I couldn't help it. He was dying," I answered.

"I will be on my way," interrupted van Patten. "Good-bye, my friend. You get a good rest tonight. Good-bye, young man." When van Patten left the room, the business of the day seemed somehow to be at an end.

Seekt got laboriously to his feet, shuffling past me. "I will meet you here before our ride to the palace tomorrow." Then he turned in the doorway to ask, "Where is little Cornelius?"

"With Maria," I answered.

Seekt leaned against the doorframe. White moustaches gallant, but eyes tired, he said to me, "You may have to raise this one, Steen. I don't know if I will have the time."

"Sir . . ." I began, but he was gone.

I wandered out. As I passed through the gardens behind the kitchen, I peered through the windows. Maria was rocking the boy in her lap in front of a low fire. His bruised arm was around her neck; I think he was sleeping. Down the lawn, in the rose garden where the blooms were just beginning to come, a figure moved. Slow and stately in the light of the moon, from bush to bush, trellis to trellis. I knew it was Katje when I saw a breeze fan out her hair. Her hair, in the moonlight, was silver and gold.

"The lady in black," I said softly, walking down the grassy allèe to where she waited for me. "Are you in mourning, lady?"

She didn't answer, but turned away from me. Then, "Steen, you're such a boy, still."

"Come for a walk," I said.

"Tell me about your visit," she said, standing with an air of resolution.

I told her about seeing Jan. She didn't move from where she stood, running her finger along the edge of a thorn.

"Come for a walk," I said when I had finished.

"No, Steen." She shook me off, walking away a few paces.

"What's wrong, Katje?"

"You would be easy to be romantic about," Katje said.

"I loved you, Katje, when I saw you. Do you remember the afternoon in the freezing wind when you kissed me? Before you went to Paris? That was my first kiss, Katje," I said.

"Now it's someone else, though. I made you a wicked suggestion then, impish. You've grown quite a young man out of it and one who somehow excludes me."

She sounded French, I thought. The French disease.

"Were his wrists really cut that way?" she said.

I nodded.

"Do you want to just wear me in your self-regard, like a gown hanging in a closet? You know, that could be. Is it?" she asked.

"I don't know," I said, thinking.

"It would be sweet," she said, "and smart, but . . . Oh, we're lords and ladies with hearts. Later, when we remember all this, I wonder what it will feel like? Maybe it would be easier for me in France, where I don't know if they love anything."

In the evening light, then, we heard a thundering on the road beyond the field. We shivered. I recognized some of our people riding by, Frederick One leading, high in the saddle and looking over his shoulder. Only paces behind our party rode a band of militia, seven or eight of them, with two pistols they discharged. Katje and I ran for the gates to the drive. We each took one side, waiting. The thunder grew louder as they rounded the bend. Then our folks clattered down the drive to the stable yard. They had just enough of a lead to enable Katje and me to swing the huge gates closed in the faces of the militia, dust and wind swirling around us. We dropped the iron crossbar into place. Militia horses reared, kicking the gates once or twice outside, their iron shoes making an awful din on the thick wood. Then a sharp knock as a pistol was fired into the gate. Amid the thrashing of horses outside, voices rose, screaming, "We'll be back, friends. We'll be back." And then the militia rode off down the road into the city.

Matt ran to us as Katje and I were shaking off the dust.

"I'm going to the French embassy for some soldiers, Matt," Katje said. "Get my horse, then go tell my father what's happened. Ask Lise to sit up with him if he's restless," she said as Matt ran to the stables. I pressed her hand.

"Be careful, will you," I said.

Then Katje was off, leaping barefoot onto her horse. Matt opened the gate for her, closed it, and ran for the house.

I went to our friends as they dismounted in front of the stables. I could see Peter, Christian, and several I didn't know bunching around Frederick One, so I guessed he had been hit. When I got there they were bandaging and tying off his left upper arm. One boy was leading the horses into their stalls, and as I ran up Frederick One called to me through his grimace, "They made a hit, Steen. First blood. Except for the executions." He spat, viciously.

"Stand still," said Peter, who was tying up the bandage, making a tight knot. Christian offered Frederick a flask of something, and when that was refused, drank from it himself.

"Can you move your arm?" asked a boy with a headband like a pirate's around his head.

"Yes, it moves fine," said Frederick.

"We are lucky," said Peter, "the bullet passed through. We can clean it upstairs."

At this, we made for the door to quarters. We all caused an enormous commotion on those little stairs.

Seven boys, Frederick One, and me. Making either eight boys or nine, depending on what you made Frederick's age to be. They all went for the cupboards, opening cheeses, getting wine, while I lighted candles. Peter and Christian set about opening the bandage all over again, pouring in some of Christian's brandy and cleaning the wound. The chomping and smacking of lips from boys around the room were interrupted by copious swearing from Frederick as the alcohol entered his wound. I went to the fireplace, black and ashen in the dim light, and stared into its darkness. A scene flashed into my mind. In the midst of all this I was for an instant back in the prison yard watching Moenen's anguished form dashing away.

Frederick stopped shouting, and I turned to face them all.

"What's the situation here?" asked Frederick, as Peter and Christian went for some food. "Do we defend? Are they coming back?"

"Katje went for the French troops," I said, "as soon as you got here. They should be back before the mob arrives, I think. That will make us safe enough through the night."

Frederick pondered this, working his injured arm and grunting. "What about the prison? What are our chances there?" he asked.

"No good. Not tonight, anyway." Some of the faces were disappointed, so I took a firm tone. "The Prins Nassau, the royal prince, is going to take a hand in this. He's helping us, and that could save us all, put an end to the whole thing. Tomorrow, Seekt and I will visit him and try to persuade him to stop the trials. While he is involved, the prins wants no illegalities, no trouble from us. We can't attack the jail. Not tonight. If the prins won't save Jan, if he doesn't agree tomorrow, then we may try the jail tomorrow night. It would be hard, though. Jan's window is only the size of a Bible."

"Shit," said one of the boys, "and we risked our skins to get here."

"Until tomorrow night," I answered, "the best thing is to win the prins's support. That's first. Then, maybe there will be no need to rescue Jan. Maybe the see will be safe then, too. Maybe the prins can stop the persecutions." I tried to be bright about this, but received no hopeful looks in return. Instead, sullen ones. Except Christian's eyes, which were assuming the amused and foggy look of a drinker. "What happened to you on the road?" I asked, changing the subject. "What's going on in the country?"

"Militia swarming all over the place," Peter answered. "Our last good road is gone; that party you saw was posted on it waiting for us tonight. There's a barricade there now too." A chill wafted through the room in the April night. "And the people," Peter continued, "villagers and farmers, take it as a holiday, time off for sport. Go heckle a few city queers. Their farm hands stop sucking each other off and run down the road to jeer at homosexuals. They've been shooting."

"We don't expect an outright attack yet," said Frederick, "because they've just begun digging trenches in the field opposite us. It will take them a while to get in place, and get their courage up. We have Peter's cannon prominently displayed," Frederick laughed. "Every day we do some practice firing. I hope that keeps them off, so we never have to really use it." At that, the boys stated their desire to use the cannon extensively, and soon. Frederick said, "No, no. Killing *is* a crime. Killing *is* in the Commandments. I want us to stay on the right side of justice. But it looks bad, Steen, it looks like there's going to be violence. I don't know." He looked at the floor.

"We are dug in and ready out there," said Peter. "We're actually pretty heavily armed, aren't we?" Vigorous nods all around.

Suddenly Frederick came to himself, remembering something. "Johann," he said, addressing the boy in the pirate headband, "go down to the gate to wait for Meister. Make sure he gets in." The boy departed. As Johann hurried past me I saw that he carried a pistol in his belt. Most of them did.

"Who is Meister?" I asked.

"He is our spy," said Frederick. "Let me tell you. One night I was out on the border with the sentries. We heard shouting, and saw a lone rider, hooded, making for our land as if his life depended on it. Behind him were a bunch of militia, shouting, closing in on him. He took our fence in a magnificent jump. I let him pass. We fired over the pursuers' heads, and they rode away. The man turned out to be a member of the cardinal's staff named Meister. A German. He said he had decided he had to help us, hadn't known there was such danger. He's to meet us here tonight."

Wine was passed around as we waited for the German. With no action imminent, the boys were going to get drunk. I thought of Katje in a formal garden, noble and sad on the arm of some French fop. I wanted to see her barefoot again; I wanted to talk to her. But all was silent outside; no French soldiers yet. Would it be the soldiers or the mob who arrived first? Then I heard the gate banging closed, and soon the sounds of boots on the stairs. The pirate came in, followed by Meister.

Meister was invisible under a peaked hood and heavy cloak until he removed them to reveal a young, freckled face and an outfit of the most somber velvets in browns and blacks. As he took off the cloak some greetings went up from the boys, who evidently liked him. Meister waved, and then came over to me. I liked him immediately.

"I am the cardinal's secretary," he explained. "He is a cousin of my family in Bavaria, and they sent me to apprentice with him for a while. I hate the cardinal." Meister smiled at me. He was about to say more, but Frederick had questions, so Meister said he would speak to me later.

"What news?" Frederick was saying. "What news?"

Meister turned to face the group. "The cardinal plans a twofold victory, a victory on two fronts in two quick stages. He's on his way to an inquisitorship in Spain, you see. But I'll explain that later. First, the double stroke. Day after tomorrow he plans to try to indict and convict Jan at trial, in one day. He wants to burn him that afternoon. He thinks this would crush his only powerful opposition in the city," said Meister, nodding in my direction, "and pave the way for the next day's action, which involves all of you. Part two is an attack on the farm out there—"

"The see," interrupted Christian, chuckling.

"Yes. Militia and drunken, bribed countryfolk will move against you the day after the trial. The cardinal wants prisoners. He wants you *all* prisoner, and he has told the captains that it is all right if there is a certain amount of killing."

"*That* there may be," said Frederick, gloomily.

"What's this about Spain?" asked Peter.

"The inquisitor general in Spain is a very powerful man," said Meister. "He usually has his way with their weak monarchs, and with a good deal of gold from their colonies as well. My uncle, as cardinal inquisitor, could build himself a heavenly mansion in Rome, and maybe someday wear three crowns. But first, the inquisitorship.

For that, he wants to prove himself a scourge to the wicked and a conqueror of vice. This week should make his name for him, and then it's off to Spain."

"You see why we must win this trial," I said. They all nodded.

"We could break it up," said a boy, belching, but Meister explained to him that that might serve the cardinal's purposes. Also, there would probably be a lot of deaths if we did that.

Frederick said, "Well, Steen, we'll stay here until you tell us what the prins decides tomorrow. Then we'll either have to rescue Jan tomorrow night, or—"

"Or leave it to us, and a legal victory," I said.

"And break through to the see tomorrow night, to start preparing *our* defense," Frederick finished. Everyone nodded. "If the trial comes out our way," Frederick asked Meister, "will the cardinal still go ahead and attack us the next day?"

"All the harder," replied Meister. "But there is one consolation in all this. My uncle is a vain and vigorous man. He rides superbly well, very strongly. He should have been a soldier. He plans to take part in the action himself. He's thrilled about it. So we'll get a shot at him."

"We?" inquired Peter.

"Yes. I'm staying with you from now on," said Meister, smiling. The boys gathered around him, patting his back, giving him drinks. I paced. Frederick brooded. Meister disengaged himself and came over to my side. Together we began walking down the long row of beds in the dark. I waited for him to speak.

"The cardinal," he began, "wants also to leave his church here richer than it was when he found it. He has been worming secrets about your family's businesses out of your twin brother for some time. And of course he's wanted to set you against each other. Do you know how he got his hold over your brother?"

"I thought they were friends," I said.

"At first, yes," he replied. "But the cardinal wanted power over Moenen. It was simple. He ordered two of his valets to seduce Moenen, and then walked in on them one night. The boys were quite willing, of course. It must have been a welcome change from the cardinal's withered old frame."

"The cardinal likes boys?" I asked.

"Yes," he laughed.

"Poor Moenen," I said. "But why not tell me? Why stay with the cardinal?"

"Moenen has fears. The cardinal played on them. He said Moenen would be ruined in the city if word leaked out. What would people think? Moenen came under the cardinal's thumb."

"Oh, Meister," I said, "if only he'd talked with me." Right then I had to get home to Moenen.

Suddenly there were sounds of shouting outside, and we all flew downstairs.

It was the French troops. Katje was standing by her horse in the courtyard as they stacked their rifles. There were at least thirty of them, their white uniforms a blur as they scurried through the night under the moon. Orders were being called out. French is an odd language to hear orders in.

I went to Katje. She was rocking slightly, back and forth on her bare feet, as she watched the Frenchmen.

"I've got to go see Moenen," I said into her ear. "He's been blackmailed by the cardinal all this time."

She replied, her eyes still on the French, but her hand moving into mine, "I'm going to go and be with Father. You had better hurry. I think there's a mob not far from here."

"Can they hold them?" I asked quickly.

"These men? Oh, yes, but there will be jeering. You have an important day tomorrow at the palace, so I'd better give Father something to sleep."

"I'll see you in the morning. Tell your father I'll meet him here. I love you." I ran for the stables. On the way, I shouted to Frederick that I was going home and I'd see them here the next day before Seekt and I left. As I clattered through the courtyard, two white French apparitions pulled the gates apart for me. As I passed the gate, I saw a line of at least twenty Frenchmen forming, muskets at the ready, outside. I was already racing down the road when I saw a glow in the distance and heard shouting. The mob. They were staggering forward, torchbearers in the lead, and when they saw me they began to throw rocks. A stone flew over my shoulder, smashing a window in a house. I veered into a side street. My heart beat very fast all the way home.

Our house was dark when I pulled in. I gave my horse to the ostler and ran through the front door, straight up the stairs to Moenen's room and in without knocking. He wasn't there.

CHAPTER SEVEN

I WOKE in my own rooms, the sun already high and bright. Birds were well into a chorus, calling to one another in the cool morning. The coming day rushed against my mind in pictures. There was a carriage ride with Seekl dozing beside me; there was the long vista of the prins's ballroom, that bald head shining at the other end; but first, there was the search for my brother. I cooked some tea and burned a biscuit, then dressed in riding clothes, since I didn't know where my search would take me. After dressing, I packed a bag with finery for our visit to the prins, some of my best lace and a new suit of sky-blue silk. This done, I ran for my brother's room, hoping he would have come in during the night. I knocked. There was no answer. I tried the knob, pushing the door open. Moenen was lying on the floor, still dressed, his clothes wrinkled from the night before. I knelt beside him. The smell told me that he had been drinking. Knowing the symptoms of that, I poured a glass of water from his basin so that he could irrigate his dry mouth when I woke him. I shook him gently.

"Don't," he croaked, eyes still shut. He moved his arms to cover his face.

I smoothed his hair. "Moenen, Moenen." He opened his eyes and looked at me with a twitching of the eyebrows. He smacked his mouth open and closed several times. Finally, he said, "Water." I had it ready. He drank, and I loosened his clothes and pulled off his stockings. I got him into a chair in sitting position. His face began to sweat, and he stared at the ceiling. After a few deep breaths and more water, he said, "I stayed out a little late last night. Don't know how I got home."

"Moenen, what's the cardinal been doing to you? I talked to his secretary yesterday. Moenen, why didn't you tell me?"

"Tell you? Ha! That was the point, not telling anyone. Tell you what?"

"That the cardinal had caught you in the act. That he was blackmailing you."

"Oh, Steen, who cares now. It's all ruined now anyway. I am afraid of mother finding out. And if they knew in the city, how would I be thought of? I *have* to keep it quiet. Meister told you? Who else did he tell?"

"No, Moenen, that's not it. He didn't tell anyone. Why do you care?"

No response.

"Do you mean," I said, "you have gone through this whole business, you've endured all this, for that? How could you, Moenen? Why didn't you talk to me sometime?"

"Oh, you ... you ..." he said, not speaking to me exactly, but speaking to some interior of his own. "You've always known; you've always done things. You've been the one all the time; you get everything. I'm sick of you. I'm sick of your advice. I did what I thought was best."

"But to be made a victim like that? How could you have let him do it?"

He was still sitting limply, talking toward the ceiling, sweat seeping from his pores. "I couldn't face people knowing what I did in bed, what I did for fun. And he said he'd tell. It was impossible. It would ruin everything; I had to go along. I couldn't have vulgar people thinking about me. It's disgusting, and now it's all ruined anyway."

"But Moenen," I said, "what do you care what they think? How can you know what anyone is going to think? And what does it matter?"

"It matters, it matters. Can I help that? I was afraid."

"Yes, and that's what gives the cardinal his opportunity for things like this. Somebody's afraid, somebody cares what somebody thinks."

"How did you ever get to be so smart, Steen?"

"Oh, Moenen, it just makes sense. I didn't learn it anywhere—I've just been happier not caring about them. It seems better than living in fear all the time. Well, doesn't it?"

"Don't know, Steen. I don't know." Here he belched so deeply that he almost vomited, and sweat really popped out on his forehead.

He began to look very ill, yet I had to ask, even then, "Moenen, what were you doing at the jail last night? I was there and I saw you leaving as I arrived. What did you do—" I was interrupted as a copious gush of vomit shot from his mouth, plopping all over the front of him and landing on the floor between us. Then he ran to his water stand and continued to be sick. I decided to leave him and let the question wait. Before going, though, I helped him swab down a little. Wordlessly, I wiped the sweat off his forehead. He stood up, breathing deep, ragged breaths. I said I'd talk with him more before the trial, and in the meantime with our friends, to see what help we could devise for his own predicament. I patted his head and left him, hoping I hadn't been callous.

Then I was off to Seekt's. It was a gray noon, perfect for all I was feeling. I knew, I *knew* we had to be successful with the prins, and so I was full of impatience. It seemed the best way I could help Moenen and Jan and all of us was to plead our case well with the Prins Nassau that day.

As I neared Seekt's neighborhood, riding on the most direct road to his house, I encountered a band of a dozen ruffians of the most hateful sort. They seemed to be out to persecute someone. They had clubs with them and bottles of liquor; they wore dirty clothes and had dirty hair. They were ambling aimlessly along singing "We Are de Witt's Boys," a rabble-rousing song of years before.

I had to pass through them, and I decided to try to make it look as if I were on my way into the countryside, not headed for Seekt's. The bag I had packed with my finery would help give this impression, so I slowed down confidently to pass through their midst. As I was trotting among them, two fellows grabbed my horse's head. I was not surprised, but I was careful to be gentle with the high-spirited horse so he wouldn't take fright and trample them. The animal shook his head smartly, which amused them, but stopped as I palmed his long neck. They gathered around us.

"This lad doesn't drink in the morning, Gus," called one to another. His hair had straw sticking out in places, and he held up a sack of wine. Chilly wind blew at me from the gray sky. "He doesn't drink at all, does he? Nice lad like you. You want to pass? Huh? Do you, lad?"

"I'm on my way," I called down, smiling at him with sympathetic amusement.

"Is it so important you can't stop for a drink with us?" said a boy. Already he had deep creases around his mouth, though I could tell that he was about my age.

"It's my girl in the country," I replied. How could they fail to understand?

"Let's get him loaded for her, huh?" shouted an older man. He had one eye, the other was a sewn wound.

"What about that?" said the young man, taking a firm hold on my leg above the stirrup.

"I'd like to stay, but I can't. You see—"

"Oh, the hell he would," shouted one-eye, "you with a horse like this, stay with us. Ha!"

"Oh, you don't know," I said, reaching for the nearest sack of wine. I drank from it, and they laughed lewdly. Then I drank again, long swallows. They became still as they watched me. I wiped my mouth with my sleeve, but held onto the sack. With my eyes temporarily out of focus from the strong drink, I said, "Well, she's going away today, and if there *is* going to be a baby, then I want her to see me decent." They laughed again, though not on my side yet, until I finished. "Because it's the last time she'll ever see *me!*" And with that I roared a cynical laugh. They joined me.

"One more drink for you then," said one-eye. "It'll cost you one more swallow." I drank again and handed back the sack.

"Ride me first. The price is a ride," said the young man, jumping up behind me on the horse's rump.

"Hey," I shouted, "all right!" Great verve. I wheeled around to go back in the other direction, so I would not have to let him down at Seekt's gate. The gang cheered as the two of us surged back toward town. As I took a turn, out of their view, the young man lost his hold and fell to the stones. I pulled around and was down beside him in a second. But all he seemed to have suffered was embarrassment. As we mounted again, he showed a limp in one leg, but he wouldn't acknowledge it, perversely using that leg all the harder to jump up from. I put the horse into a respectable but slow gait on our way back.

"Fine, jumpy horse you have," he said, right into my ear, because he was riding with both arms around my waist.

"Where are you going today?" I asked.

"Oh, those butt-boys at the end of the road here . . . we're going to go rough up those butt-boys. There's a whole nest of them down the road here." We came in view of his friends again. "Make him prance now," he asked, so I urged the horse to a smart gait. As we came among them, the gang cheered. "And tomorrow," he said as he sidesaddled to jump down, "we're going to burn one of 'em in town."

He pushed off the side of me getting down, so I was nearly off balance as I spurred the horse and made a straight wake through them in a very sudden gallop. By the time I was nearing Seekt's gate they were lost to view, far down the road.

The mob opposite Seekt's was quite large by this time. I rode directly through the French pickets, straight to their captain. As I presented myself, the crowd pushed forward toward our side, shouting and cursing. It sounded ugly, serious, heartless. As the captain signaled the opening of the gate, I admired those white-garbed Frenchmen who could keep such a monster at bay. Dismounting in the courtyard, I saw Seekt's carriage standing ready. The boys from the country were crowded around the door of the house, and I ran up to them. Frederick One and Meister greeted me first. My eyes went to the bandage on Frederick's arm.

"We'll wait for your return from the prins before we make any move, Steen," said Frederick. "But remember, we may be needed sometime at the see."

Peter edged through the crowd on the porch. "We are breaking out muskets from Seekt's collection, Steen."

"Going hunting today. Everybody but me," came a voice. It was Christian, curly hair, eyes blurred as he stumbled to me. He was so far gone that I looked at Peter with alarm.

"Scared," muttered Peter, big Peter, watching his friend.

I went inside to find Seekt. Some of the boys were sitting

cross-legged on the shiny tile floor, oiling guns and bagging powder. Katje met me at the top of the stairs. We stood apart, looking at each other. Irony and admiration as we looked.

"He's sick, Steen," she said. "He didn't sleep." And in answer to my eyes then, she added, "But he's going. He's dressed. I'll get him downstairs if you'll promise to hide the guns so he won't see them."

I nodded and went to speak to Frederick and Peter. Soon the little arsenal had been carried into the courtyard and out of view.

"Call Matt. Tell him Seekt and I are going," I said to a boy, then I shouted up the stairs, "Ready, Katje."

When she appeared, Seekt was with her. She held his arm, and he kept his hand on the banister as he descended, step by slow step. I ran to the yard and shouted to the boys, "No sight of guns. That disturbs him." So they all milled about on the grass, empty-handed. When Seekt appeared in the doorway, Lise on one side and Katje on the other, the boys cheered, "Hurray for Seekt! Yay, Seekt!" they yelled, looking up at him. Seekt beamed at us, eyes twinkling. He dropped the girls' arms and advanced by himself, shaking almost imperceptibly, down the stairs to the coach. Matt took his place on the box and quickly we were away. I shut out the sounds of the jeering crowd, and when I turned I saw Seekt staring ahead of him, at the front of the carriage, like a man shocked into silence by the sight of a great painting. He was breathing hard, but regularly. His eyes bulged a little.

"How are you, Herr Seekt?" I asked, but he did not seem to hear. When the question had died, and I had given it up, he turned, fixed his eyes on me, and said, "I'm all right, Steen. I have a little time left. We'll see the prins today."

My mind blanked. I was frightened, but I put it aside. I gazed from the window, listening to his heavy breathing. Soon the awful marshes appeared, and we were on the road to the prins's. Then I remembered. "Herr Seekt! I forgot my good clothes!"

"He will not mind, boy. I think he would prefer you this way. Remember, he has seen a lot of finery in his day, finery that put most mortal efforts to shame. Forget about it." He patted my knee. He patted it a long time, so long that I became embarrassed, until I realized that he was looking away, lost in his own thoughts, patting my knee like a man stroking a cat while he muses.

Just before we reached the long lines of poplars which finally hid the marsh, Seekt began to snore. I worried what condition he would be in to greet his old friend, but realized that I had better let him sleep as long as he could. I even wondered if I should go in alone, to let Seekt sleep.

The ramparts of the prins's palace appeared, cannon muzzling through the embrasure of the ancient forecourt. We passed on to the elegant, double-bow staircase and French facade of the newer section. As soon as the carriage jolted to a halt, Seekt's eyes popped open and he seemed more awake than he had all day.

"Mary!" said Seekt, "it's been a long time since I was here." All his bulk lurched down from the carriage. "What days were here once, Steen! When Charles of England dined here—oh, the times." He was on the raked gravel, standing smartly with cane and paunch, leaning back to survey the sandstone facade stretching beyond vision, it seemed, down the horizon. I stood with him while a footman waited for us at the bottom of one of the staircases. When at last we started our climb, Seekt was quite steady. He plodded a bit, and kept hard by the stone railing. At the top, he turned like a sightseer to view the courtyard below, but as I watched him breathing I knew the real purpose of his delay. When he had gotten his breath, he turned around just in time to see the great entrance doors, wrought iron and glass a story and a half tall, swing open like ships' prows cutting the waves. We each breathed deeply, Seekt and I, as we crossed into the shadow of the hall.

In the darkness, Seekt's cane rapped on the marble tiles. Then I saw that the footman was leading us on a different way from the route of my previous visit. I was thankful. Perhaps Seekt would be spared an endless promenade. We turned down a short corridor, and then, to our left, the footman threw open two doors and stood at stiff attention waiting for us. Just before we reached the entrance, Seekt paused. He drew himself up. A calmness washed over his face. He breathed deeply, but comfortably, staring ahead.

"Our prince," he said to me, and we strode in. Seekt's

walk was careful and after a few steps he made that low, sweeping bow of the kind hardly seen any more. I imitated it as best I could.

This was a much smaller room than the ballroom, a salon, with turquoise walls, molding of gold, and one crystal chandelier. At the other end, by windows that let in the weak light of that cloudy day, stood the prins. He wore the same velvet gray I'd seen him in before. The bald head shining, the faultless lace, and black shoes shiny as mirrors; these were things I remembered.

"My friend," he said as we advanced. He held out his left hand until he had grasped Seekt's arm, and then he steered Seekt toward the window; the shiny monkey leading the bear. "What have we not done, old friend? There . . ." He swept his arm toward the outside view. "Do you remember when Czar Peter told me one hot afternoon that the drive lacked only poplar trees to make this a beautiful view? Ah."

"And the next morning, a hundred and twenty of them were planted there," replied Seekt.

"Smaller then, were they not?" said the prins.

When the two stood together for some minutes, wordlessly, it seemed the world stood still. A clock ticked down the hall, the heartbeat of a world one never got to know. The prins sighed, and without turning from their view, still facing the windows alongside Seekt, he made a quick motion with his hand behind him indicating that I should join them.

"I see," he was saying to Seekt, "that you have brought young Steen on the second of his visits to me. That was kind of you."

"We have come to seek your advice, my lord," said Seekt. "Steen's friend is on trial, on some charge of personal misconduct. It is in an impromptu court arranged by Cardinal Inez de Bourgos, who wishes to become the grand inquisitor one day." During this, I could see neither of the two men, since we all stood in a line gazing out at the view of formal gardens bounded by poplars.

"I have heard of it. The country is in a furor over it, or so I believe," said the prins. *At last.* I knew I should not speak; I held my breath. "So he wishes to lubricate his way to Madrid with Dutch blood. Is that it, my friend?" said the prins to Seekt.

"I fear that we are on the verge of bloodshed, yes. Groups are arming." I was dying to steal a look at the prins when Seekt said that, but the formality of the scene held me stiff and proud. I remembered Peter on his cannon.

"Does the situation touch you, my old friend, or your interests?" asked the prins in a gentle hiss.

"I am a small target, Your Highness, but I am safe. Louis's dispensation allows me a guard of French dragoons . . . if you remember."

The prins smiled. I could feel the smile. "I will send you a contingent of *my* men today to replace them," said the prins.

"Thank you, sir," said Seekt without softening his tone.

The veiled sun moved in the prins's formal garden, clouding one after another of the box-bush shapes.

"But someday, one of these executions of His Eminence's will get out of hand," continued Seekt, "and we will give Europe a nice Dutch riot to gabble about."

"Your instincts have always been good," said the prins. "You think it is time we took a hand?"

Seekt nodded. Words would have been less effective.

The prins said, "I will summon the cardinal next week and hand him a letter which he may deliver in person to my cousin the king of Spain. When he is gone, a simple decree will suffice for his impromptu court."

I couldn't restrain myself. It wasn't a matter of thought —suddenly I was at the prins's feet. I couldn't touch him, grasp him about the knees as supplicants do. Something about his presence, whether age or such unnatural cleanliness, made that impossible. But I was on my knees before him, saying, "Please, please, couldn't you possibly do it in time to—"

Seekt interrupted, lifting me in his big arm. "Forgive us, sir. The boy is young." On my feet, I tried to catch the prins's eye, to see what was there. But his gaze was fixed out the window in a neutral stare, as if nothing had happened.

"The fact is, sir, that my former ward, the painter now

known as Jan of Soest, is not only to be tried tomorrow, but we are told that he may almost certainly be burned. They have already burned a number of young people. Things are rising to a certain pitch. My houses in city and country are the scenes of ugliness already, and there will be other demonstrations. I don't know that violence can be avoided now. I should have come to you sooner, sir."

"Seekt," the Prins said in a clear voice, "I cannot summon the cardinal on such short notice. I can't see him tomorrow. What would you have me do?"

"Could you, sir, send a representative of your own to the trial tomorrow, to at least allow us to question the court, to make petitions on your behalf? If *you* sent someone, we could certainly get the boy released to us. That would also serve notice on the cardinal that this business is over. Would not that be the most practical approach in any case?"

"I think you're right, Seekt. That would be a most effective prelude to my invitation to the cardinal . . . yes. Who should carry my writ to the court?"

"Have you a legal adviser or a secretary who could come tomorrow?" asked Seekt.

"Anyone in my livery could do the thing, as long as he can read aloud. But I have always been fond of irony, of a close hit," said the prins. "Perhaps young Steen has recovered sufficiently to suggest a good candidate. Whom would he suggest?"

In my eyes, in that moment, the whole formal garden was tinged with gold as I prepared to participate in my own salvation. I ruled the world as I stood weighing, wondering, making my choice. I did not want to do it myself. There was no virtue in that, only stage fright. Then I thought who could do it, and the clock down the hall echoed his name.

"Moenen should do it," I said clearly.

Although I couldn't see the other two as we stood in line at the windows, I could feel the prins's bewilderment. Seekt explained, "Moenen is Steen's twin brother, sir. Did you know that Konrad van Leuwen had twin sons? The twin, Moenen, has been roped into serving on that very court.

"It would, of course," continued Seekt to me, "be a mark

of special favor to your family, were the prins to raise your brother from magistrate to royal representative—"

"It appeals to me," cut in the prins. "I like the idea of picking one of their own to announce their demise." He turned from the window. "Take your ease, Herr Seekt. I will have them serve you something. Rest, and look out on the fields of our youth. Look where once there were no flowers, and remember how they grew betimes," said the prins, pulling a chair for Seekt and patting him into it. Then he walked to a door in the corner, indicating that I should follow. "My library," he whispered.

Library indeed! It was two stories high, a rectangular room. Three of the walls were all bookshelves, and in the fourth was a great window with square panes, except at the top, which was rounded. A narrow balcony ran above for access to the upper shelves. I saw that all the thousands of books were bound in gray leather, with only the prins's crest and the title stamped on the spine in gold. He walked to a long, graceful desk that stood under the window. He summoned a footman, gave orders for Seekt's refreshments, then turned to me.

"Do you know how dynasties survive, how they get along?" he said to me.

"No, sir."

His bald head glittered under the window, his gray suit whispered in the light reflected from the rich wood of the desk. "We grant favors, and then ask favors in return." I waited. "Your friend Jan will visit me here one week from today, at three o'clock, as you have done." His strangely youthful, moist eyes glittered at me. "I ask you to tell only him, and tell no one else."

I bowed. It felt like a perfectly graceful bow without any effort on my part. Now I knew what it really meant to bow to a prince.

A secretary was summoned, and the prins turned from me to dictate. I was left to admire the library. When they were finished the secretary came to me, bowed, and proffered a rolled parchment with a blue ribbon tied around it, heavy at one end because of the large wax seal there. When we were alone again, the prins said, "You should deliver that to your twin. Being a van Leuwen, he need not know its contents beforehand. Your family has read our writ often enough before. Your twin will do well. This instrument announces to the court that your friend is to be freed and that the court is suspended for the present. Since you conducted yourself with honor in the matter of our letter of mark, I trust you will devise a proper way of delivering this instrument tomorrow."

"Thank you, sir. Thank you very much," was all I said.

We walked back to Seekt. They looked at each other for a long time, smiling, until Seekt, leaning heavily on his cane, bowed before the prins. The prins's youthful eyes were darting beyond Seekt's back, searching the corners of the room. Seekt rose again to his full height.

"You are welcome here at any time, young Herr van Leuwen. Remember that. And remember my message to your friend." Seekt turned his gaze on me as if we shared a secret I had not known before then. We both bowed again briefly, and the prins stood in his window bay while we walked at Seekt's slow pace out of the room.

"Herr Seekt," the prins called, when we had reached the doors. "Where *did* you find all those poplars that hot summer night?"

Seekt turned around slowly; and he smiled at the prins, a slow, thoughtful smile, eyes twinkling. Neither man said a word, only smiled at each other until Seekt, then I, turned away.

Slowly, we reached the great entrance hall, under whose marble arches so much must have happened. There, two men in the prins's blue awaited us. Between them, lying on the floor, was a finely wrought wicker litter.

"For me, gentlemen?" Seekt said, approaching it. They stayed stiff, at attention, and he climbed into it, immense relief showing in a smile that lifted his white moustaches. They carried him outside, down one loop of the double-bow stairs at a beautiful angle. Like a barge cresting gentle waves, down the sandstone stairs Seekt bobbed. After he'd entered the carriage, the litter was put up on the box with Matt. The two footmen climbed on the back of the coach for the trip home, telling Matt exactly how he must drive. The gray afternoon grew pink from the west, a little, with April's early sunset. April 29, 1729.

After some time, I made bold.

"Where *did* you get all those poplars for the prins in one night?"

Casting a look out the window, Seekt answered, "From the czar."

"But wasn't it the czar who suggested them? Wasn't he staying with the prins?"

"He was staying, yes. A hot summer day. In the late afternoon the czar, after hunting, wondered why the newly French estate did not have poplars to line its drive. The prins was taken by surprise, and that wasn't good. But I knew of a ship riding at anchor in Amsterdam full of a most remarkable cargo—quantities of poplar trees, sacked for shipment to Russia. It happened to be a ship of mine. So it was no trouble to go down to the wharf that night and get the trees. I got some wagoneers to ride them out to the palace. A harbor master was induced to believe that the ship, when it sailed that night, sailed full of living lumber for Russia. In fact, I just sent her elsewhere for cargo. The trees were dug in by dawn, and the workers vanished. The prins loves to make a prank, but it has been *my* joke alone all these years that the trees were for shipment to Russia, paid for by Czar Peter, for a new city in Russia which he named after himself. Nobody ever knew that they were his own trees. When the czar wondered at the poplars the next morning, he didn't know they were his own. But I knew. And when he arrived home in the swamps of his new city, which he thought of as a northern Venice, I had to notify him that his cargo had been lost. I wrote telling him that I was making him up another, out of the best French trees. And I did."

"Wasn't it expensive?"

"No. I had tax favors from the prins that year for various reasons, and when my ship picked up a returning Russian cargo of malachite, I was able to arrange such a handsome sale that the trees were more than paid for. When they remember that summer, several old heads in Europe wonder where the Prins Nassau's tree-lined drive appeared from one night that summer. But I know."

Late afternoon was fading into early evening and the new leaves overhead broke up the last sun of the day. I looked up through the carriage window to see showers of gold sifting through the canopy of trees. In my lap was the parchment; sun glittered there as if the parchment were just an object among other objects. Its mottled, sinuous white texture blended with the flashes of sunlight and there rose from the thing a vision of us all set free, of youths running into a summer field. I imagined a reign of beauty, a plutocracy of the uncompromised, wine and challenges served to us by angels, summer evenings that found us still alive, drowsy, as the corpse of August licked our hands.

I heard screaming. The crowd, maybe fifty people opposite Seekt's gate, was swelling toward the white line of guards. When the guards fired above their ears, the people receded. I prayed that the prins's men got there before any bloodshed; we couldn't have French killing Dutch in Amsterdam. We rode in without incident. Through the window, I told the French captain about the prins's promise of replacements.

"Eh bien, meinherr," he said, *"le Roi s'en soit fort content";* I believe he said. The captain helped Seekt into the litter, the sight capturing everyone's attention as the prins's two footmen carried Seekt up the steps. Katje, wearing a blue dress, waited for her father and followed him inside. Frederick One and Peter and Meister and the other boys encircled me quietly; Maria stood beyond the circle, holding Cornelius's hand.

I held up the parchment. "A decree to destroy the court. Where should we keep it?" There was a moment of silence. It roared louder than any cheering.

"If *you* keep it," Frederick said to me, "you'll have to stay here and be prepared to escape with it if necessary."

"I'm going to my house," I answered, "so I can take it home. Getting to court with it in the morning is no problem if I am able to get it home safely tonight. What will you all do?"

"I'm going to court in the morning. I want to see my father," said Peter.

"The rest of us had better go back to the see." Frederick looked at me with concern as he said this, wondering whether he should take everybody back at once.

"You'll get through," I answered. Wind kept the French

a long time at lighting their wet wood. "Try not to hurt anyone. Perhaps it will end tomorrow."

"I wouldn't predict that, knowing my uncle's plans," said Meister.

"I wouldn't predict that, knowing the militia," said a boy.

"Be prudent," I said to Frederick.

"We've been!" he shouted. "You know that big woman with the bracelet, the Earth Mother? Between cannon practice, she comes out and serves the hecklers gingerbread and tells us all that it can't, it simply can't come to blows. We've been prudent."

"All right, all right," I said, gazing down at his boots.

"So we're going back and hold the fort," said Frederick. "Will you send us word immediately about the trial tomorrow?"

"I will," I promised.

As the boys went for their horses, I had a sudden thought. I ran to them and said, "Wait until I talk to Katje for a few minutes. Then, if you ride out the gate, I can escape under your cover, after you've distracted the crowd. Will you wait for me?"

"Fine," Frederick said. "I want it to be completely dark when we reach the barricades anyway. We'll wait here."

I ran into the house. Katje was leaving her father's room, and motioned for me to be quiet. We went downstairs silently and then I said, "So my brother will get to put the mud in their eye himself, and show them that a van Leuwen is not easily played with." She looked at me. "Are you going to call the doctor for your father?"

"He won't have doctors. He mixes herbs himself, says he refuses to be treated by doctors. This morning, he told me how long he will live." Katje said this easily, making me take the whole weight of the emotion.

"Will it be long?" I asked levelly. She shook her head.

"I had mail from France today," she said then, without taking her eyes from mine. I looked away. My stomach became jumpy.

"Is that lawyer coming?" I asked, looking over her head.

"What? Oh, no, he never wrote back to me. This was from the viscomte who loves me," she said, with her orphaned laugh.

"No, no," I was saying, holding her and swinging her back and forth. "You stay with us, please. We're going to make a magnificent life here."

"I won't see you before the trial. I'll ride with Father," Katje said. "Go safely."

"Your father will go, won't he?"

"He says he will." And Katje looked through the door behind me into the April evening.

They were waiting for me when I ran out into that dusk. They sat their horses quietly as I mounted. While I stowed the parchment in my traveling bag, Frederick and Meister watched me with care. Peter and Christian and Cornelius stood on the ground.

"We'll see you at the court tomorrow," said Peter, and I nodded.

We got a long head start out of the courtyard and the pack of us burst into full gallop on the road, riding like the Furies, Frederick crying, "Clear the way!" Through the thundering dust I saw the crowd turn after my friends on their way into the country. None of them chased me. I rode home fast, with no pursuit.

I entered the house by my own door, and hid the parchment in one of my rooms. On my way to find Moenen, I passed my mother's room. Her door was open. She sat in a lace dressing gown before a small fire, the remains of her dinner before her on a tray. She called to me and I went in and sat down opposite her. I asked if Moenen was home, knowing, somehow, that he was, and she said he was downstairs.

"I hear there is some trouble in town. Are you boys involved in that?" she asked me.

"No, Mother," I said.

"Your friend is to be tried tomorrow," she continued, looking at me closely. "Will you have him released?"

"Yes," I answered.

"Steen, I want you to be careful. You might not think it at all, when you contemplate this country, but the Dutch can be a violent people. There have been ugly times, as when they murdered the de Witt brothers. Never underestimate their rage; take care in public. Do you promise?"

I promised. I kissed her, and went looking for Moenen. Downstairs, my shoes clicked on the tiles as I crossed the hall from one dark room to another, not finding him. At last I entered the long gallery where French doors let in the first moonlight. There he was, standing in the spot where he had held court during our party last winter, at the far end, in moonlight. I paced down the gallery toward him.

"I love you, Steen," he said quietly when I was a few paces away from him. I went closer and stood facing him. "I thought I loved Jan for a time, when he was arrested. I visited him each of these nights. That's what I was doing when you saw me there. He was kind to me. Maybe it was confusing to him. I wanted to see him. I thought he was going to die. He told me I could be free of the court if I wanted to be, and I pretended he was making love to me. At night I pretended he held me like I've seen him hold you sometimes.

"But I can't stop the cardinal. Tomorrow I'm going to make a scene in that court and they will not forget it, but it will gain us only some time. Maybe he can escape. I'll help you. We will arrange it somehow."

"Moenen, it's done. I have a writ from the Prins Nassau, a decree releasing Jan and dissolving the court. We're saved, Moenen."

He shouted, and he did a little dance. I explained more.

"Will you read the decree tomorrow?" I asked. "Is there a good moment in the proceedings when you can stand up and blow them to hell?"

"Yes," he cried, taking my shoulders. "Yes! I know when. Where is the decree?"

"Upstairs. We'll take it to court together tomorrow. Let's dress like twins, all right?"

"Steen, hold me," he said, and I did. It was simple, except that our hands found each other's long hair, which shone golden in the moonlight, little rivers of dark gold curls.

After a time, we discovered that we had pushed each other back again, and were standing apart, holding each other's arms.

"Remember the bird I caught once in the country," he said, "and you made me let it go? I will do that again now, won't I? But you'll help me. I can find lots of friends now, right?"

I nodded, trying to hold him again, but he kept talking. "I'll crush them tomorrow, Steen. It will be *my* day—our day, but *my* day. Steen, we're going to be fine."

We hugged. Then I saw him to his room, and tucked him in.

As on the day before, I woke late, making up sleep from that whole furious week. It was the last day of April. When I went to Moenen's room he was standing waiting for me like a little boy. We kissed, then he said, "Court is at eleven. How shall we go?"

"In the carriage!" I said. We went downstairs together to have breakfast. We served each other. From the food laid out, each fixed the other's plate, poured the other's coffee. We had used to do that. I remember looking at his arm as he poured. Narcissus leans over the pool.

After the meal, I took him to my room to get the parchment. He said, "I'll catch your eye before I stand up. You bring it to me then."

We did not speak during the ride, and shortly our carriage pulled up to a shallow porch where the door of the court chamber stood open. A two-tiered chamber, it looked not unlike a church, except that the door opened through one of the long walls. Arched windows set high in that wall let sun onto the marble floor, which ran past rows of carved-wood benches. It was like the long choir of a cathedral, though it had always been a civil chamber. Long tiers across from the entrance were to hold the judges. All this Moenen showed me as we stood in the open door, our ears throbbing with the noise of the mob outside. Militiamen stood near the mob, arms interlocked, holding the crowd away before the building. Katje arrived as we watched, followed by four mounted soldiers of the prins's. Moenen and I went to her as she dismounted.

"My father said we could do it without him, so he would stay home and rest on his laurels," Katje said. I noticed that she avoided looking at Moenen.

"Where should these men be stationed?" I asked, indicating her escort. We decided to bring them inside the court.

Soon enough the room was filled. An audience of gentry

was present, clergymen and ladies mostly. Moenen went across the marble floor to the still empty judges' row, to the highest place, with seats roped off in front of it. He took his place just as the five other judges came in. I stood in front of the bank of benches near the door. To my right, I saw Peter and Christian sitting with lawyer van Patten. They had saved a bench for me. Katje climbed up onto it. Holding the parchment scroll against my leg, I quietly instructed the prins's escort to move, as soon as Jan was brought in, to wherever he went and to assume charge of him. They shouldered their muskets and waited. I climbed to our bench, three steps up from the marble floor.

I looked carefully at the judges. Peter's father and the mayor, I recognized. Three others were landowners, not city folk. Soon after my brother had sat down, the cardinal glided in wearing slim, scarlet robes, skullcap over his stringy white hair, holding his cross in both hands, at the ends of those bony fingers. He was laughing with a man who walked behind him. The cardinal seated himself and, with a sharp, birdlike look, signaled to a man who rang a little bell. This brought in Jan, held by two militiamen. They seated him in a chair at the foot of the hall. He looked at me. I was looking at him, and we smiled into each other's eyes. I saw that he had his gold watch, the chain across his waist.

The cardinal's bright eyes darted at the country judge who rose to announce that the court was convened and other formalities. While this was taking place, I watched Peter catch his father's eye. They stared at each other as if each were seeing a ghost. His father looked frightened in a way I can hardly describe, deeply frightened. Peter stared.

"Corrupter! Although you are only eighteen years old, you have . . ." the cardinal said as he stood up and faced Jan. But Moenen had stood up too, looking surprised, as if he hadn't meant to stand quite yet. I calmly walked across with the large scroll, holding it up to Moenen, who took it. Untying the ribbon, he said, "I must interrupt, Your Eminence. This is a decree from His Highness the Prince of Orange and Nassau, regarding these proceedings." He held up the large parchment to show them. It hung heavily where its wax seal weighed one corner. The cardinal stood gaping. Moenen held the scroll and read: "By Our will, the prisoner Jan is released, unhindered, to the care of his friends, at the hearing of these words." Our escort replaced the two confused militiamen by Jan's side. "All other prisoners held in the Netherlands by order of this court are to be released without hindrance. This court is dissolved until such time as it may be invited by Us to explain its activities. By Our hand this day . . ."

Then Moenen stood before the cardinal. With one hand behind his back, he held out the long scroll for the cardinal's inspection. The cardinal did glance at the seal, but paling, spared himself the rest. As he tried to glance away, however, one of the royal escort troops presented himself and handed the cardinal a letter, sealed. The cardinal tapped the letter deftly up his wide sleeve, then he turned and walked through the confusion and out of the court.

Suddenly I was lifted up into the air and fell back on Jan's chest. He'd spun me around from behind. We hugged very hard. Our friends surrounded us, except Moenen, who was still at the judges' side. I made room for Moenen between me and Katje when he did arrive, but Moenen iced the group. The smiles vanished. And something more; in the lull, I saw Jan and Moenen exchange a look I couldn't read. I hugged Moenen. I wanted him to be with us now, to begin to be civilized. Gradually, we all laughed a little again and smiled, and it felt all right.

So we stood by the door, triumphant youth, while the crowd filed out past us. There were more than a few hateful looks from those pinched people for whom vengeance and indignation are the mainsprings of life. We had cheated the people. Soon everyone drifted away, until Moenen and I were left standing alone in the empty hall, silent.

"Is it fun?" Moenen said into the empty room, as if speaking to someone of limited intelligence.

"What?" I asked.

Looking into my eyes, he lifted his hand in the air, palm up, before dropping it back to his side.

I went and shook his shoulders, staring into his face. "Can't you wake up? You're free now, Moenen."

"For what?"

I said, "Are you crazy? To quarrel *again* while the world offers you everything."

"Thanks, Mama," Moenen said. Then, "Where am I?"

"In Amsterdam," I told him.

Moenen smiled.

CHAPTER EIGHT

FUNNY, when I walked into Seekt's hall that night, I was thinking about hair, remembering people's hair on pillows and hair blowing in the wind. Jan came down the stairs, abstracted, in a world completely his own; as he talked to me, he looked like a man intent on a map. He was going to his studio to draw something. He said that Seekt had died in the afternoon.

I stayed in the hall, but not alone, because the house was filled with people, maids carrying clothes and linen, not crowds, but a constant movement of people darting through the hall. I walked out to the stable. There was a light far down the building, at the top, where Jan was working. I stood by the door, feeling the darkness become damp, misty, and I thought I saw the ghost of Seekt's carriage rumbling past me down the drive, the gates swing open, and imagined an angry shouting out on the road. A flash of Seekt's white hair, a rhododendron bough glistening in the night.

After a time, I went into the stable and climbed the stairs to interrupt Jan. It was a physical reunion taking place at a moment of death. We had an amazing night.

The funeral for Seekt was a few days later, at the see. On that morning, Moenen and I had breakfast together. We were mostly silent as we poured each other's coffee, eating, looking through the windows. We left home at different times, Moenen going first because he had someone to visit before heading for the country. It was fully dawn when I started out. After a time I saw a wisp of smoke down the road which told me I was near the inn. When I rounded the bend and passed the front of that building, I encountered riders from Seekt's house, making for the see. Katje was in her coach, with Seekt's casket. There were soldiers of the prins in front, and retainers. I rode behind the large group, off at a distance, listening to the sounds of low voices and horse tackle. When we arrived, everyone at the see was milling about. People moved quickly toward the chapel. Seekt's grave was dug there, under the dome.

Seekt's boarders straggled around the chapel doors. Mothers with babies formed a small crowd on the new grass by the bushes, rolling a ball back and forth for the children. The women all wore aprons as white as snow. For an instant, I thought two of the little girls were twins. They danced together in circles, arms spread, but then each ran to a different mother. I entered the dusty, swirling light of the chapel. Under Jan's mural, in the little round altar, my friends were gathered.

I made my way through the press of see folk, toward Jan and Katje and Lise, who stood together beside one of the tall candles. Peter and Christian, the two Fredericks, lawyer van Patten and his thinner companion, all of these and several boys I recognized. I passed the large, dignified woman whom Frederick One had called "our Earth Mother," the one who had prayed at dinner. There were also several dignitaries wearing ribbons or badges of rank. I saw the French ambassador.

Seekt's casket lay on boards over a hole dug in the altar floor. Sunlit motes danced in the shifting rays of sun, so that for one motionless instant, all seemed caught in a reverent still life. Matt stood. He glared as stonily at Seekt's bier as he had glared at his master alive. Only now, I saw the same gaze transferred at intervals to Katje. I pushed my way to Jan's side, simply to feel his shoulder and arm against mine. "Hello," he said quietly. I looked into his eyes.

Katje stared ahead over her father's casket. She occasionally turned to Lise, away from us, as if to talk, but she didn't say a word. She didn't cry, either. When our eyes met, it felt like lovers meeting years later. Two young guitarists stepped forward and played a gigue. A memorial was read by the French ambassador. And that was that.

Before the boys lowered the coffin under long silk

ribbons, Katje went and put her hand on the lid for an instant. Matt stood behind Katje, but nobody else moved. We were exchanging glances, looking like classmates on the last day of school. Then, we gathered into a circle, arms linked. The Fredericks, together, called firmly, "Three cheers for Seekt!" and as we cheered, "Hurrah! Hurrah! Hurrah!" tears appeared on several faces. Then we broke up, Katje leading on her way to say adieu to the ambassador.

Then Jan and I were left almost alone in the light from the tall windows at the altar, while two boys began shoveling large moist chunks of dirt over Seekt's casket. We turned away. I couldn't abide the hollow, empty knocks of the earth falling onto the lid. We looked up through the windows at the new boughs of spring outside. After a time, I managed to say, "Can we be together tonight?"

"Um," he said, holding me.

Then the door banged closed at the other end of the room, and Moenen was standing there. We both turned to look at him as he crossed the chapel toward us.

"Are you happy?" Moenen said, drawing near to me.

"Oh, Moenen," I said.

Moenen stood beside me, looking up at Jan. Their eyes flickered at each other for a minute.

Then Jan drew Moenen under his arm and hugged him, sort of sideways. It made me nervous. "See," Jan said, "I've painted you. There, up there." He took Moenen's chin and lifted it till Moenen's eyes met the figure that had our features.

"That's Steen," said Moenen, looking Jan in the eye.

Behind us we heard the sharp, metallic crunch of the boys' spades in the dirt.

"Maybe it would be your image too," Jan said to him, "if you would let some softness in your eyes."

For just a moment Moenen looked up at him like a boy. Then he turned to me, producing from under his coat the scroll that had dissolved the court only days before.

"We owe Herr Seekt a great deal, I think. I wanted to bring this, Steen," my brother said. "I think it belongs with him."

Moenen threw the parchment down into the grave and,

with a look, directed the boys to go on filling in, burying it in the moist earth. We watched as the white scroll, bright in the sunbeams, quickly disappeared under dirt with dead roots stringing out of it.

We all walked to the Fredericks' house to join the gathering there. I walked on one side of Jan, Moenen on the other. There was tension on that side, tension between them. Something was not being said. I wondered about Moenen's visits to Jan in jail.

In the Fredericks' house, people were eating and drinking. I thought Seekt would have liked it. Rumor had it that Katje had given the deed of the see to the Fredericks.

Little Cornelius was standing near Katje as she talked with the Fredericks. There was a lot of food and wine; people moved through the clear light to and from the lawn. The three of us, Moenen and Jan and I, stood aside like some organism doomed in the grand scheme of things.

"I'm going home," Moenen said after a time, turning toward the door.

"Wait, Moenen," I called. Jan took my arm as I, too, turned.

"See you at your rooms tonight?" Jan asked. I nodded and kissed him, then ran into the courtyard after Moenen.

"Let's ride over to the farm before we go back," I called to him as we mounted. "Let's go to the millpond."

As we started out, little Cornelius ran to me, grabbing at my stirrup. "Play with me," he shouted. My horse began to plunge. I reached down and ruffled his hair, patted his head, and then raced off after Moenen.

Moenen kept a distance between us during the ride; he knew I wanted to talk to him. We rode fast and hard to the farm, with Moenen edging into the lead all the way. As we passed the barricade nearest the farm, I saw that country people still lounged there, drinking, taunting the prins's troops who were bivouacked in their midst to keep order.

Once on our own land, Moenen slowed. He allowed me to catch up, and when he turned to speak the spring wind gusted in his light hair, blowing it like bird feathers.

"I'll leave you alone," he said.

"I don't understand what's happening," I said.

"Typical," said Moenen.

"You have no heart at all, do you?" I said.

"What's happening, little brother, is that I'm stealing your boyfriend without even trying," Moenen said.

"Don't, Moenen," I said.

"It's not *me*. It's just happening," Moenen said, "because he hasn't had me yet."

"Don't think too highly of yourself, Moenen," I said, looking down the road across our fields.

"Save that for strangers, little brother," his voice said.

"I'm not your little brother," I said.

"Well, you're not little," said Moenen.

"You're *wrong*, Moenen," I said, cantering the horse, Moenen bouncing beside me. "It's not just a game like that. Jan and I will be all right, Moenen."

"Will you help me in the India Company?" Moenen asked.

"Yes," I said.

"You and I are going to have to kiss Iselin's ass for some time into the future, you know," Moenen said.

There was a commotion down the thin strip of dirt through our fields. We spurred, but the other riders reached the wooden bridge before we did, so we had to move aside or be ridden down by the three galloping figures. Two lackeys were led by a crimson figure, all three racing. The cardinal's red riding cape billowed from his shoulders, almost straight into the faces of his aides. As the trio entered the bridge I saw that it was Meister riding behind his ancient master. The cardinal smashed by us, a blur of red, his stringy white hair flying free. I thought Meister smiled at me as he passed. Moenen shouted to me, "You get the aides. I'm going after the cardinal."

We turned on the road in a flash. The cardinal spurred without even looking over his shoulder; he must have sensed Moenen coming. But Meister and his companion were not so quick, and as Moenen passed them he edged them right off the road. Meister made a leisurely circle in the field of grass, so I rode to the other one first. Coming even with him, I shouted into the boy's face, "My brother wants a word with your master. Stay here." It worked; the boy looked at the ground and let his horse begin to graze. I rode out to Meister. He had a bright smile for me when I reached his side.

"We've been out to see the prins," Meister said. "Sorry about the trespass. I don't know why His Eminence chose *this* road back to Spain."

"It's the straightest route," I said, and for some reason we laughed.

Soon Moenen rode back to us.

"I caught up with him," he said, "and rode beside him for a few seconds, looking into his face. But his horse is bigger than mine. At our border I pulled up and let him go."

"Didn't you say anything?" asked Meister.

"I shouted, after he had gone by me."

"What?" Meister asked.

"I shouted, 'Live with yourself!' But the wind blew it back to me," said Moenen.

That evening, as I waited for Jan, I stood by my windows. It grows dark slowly in springtime and the dusk was pink and slow. I tried to trace it, to gauge the progress of shadows among the branches of our cherry trees. But I couldn't note precisely where the darkness crept in. It seemed that when I looked away from a certain spot and then returned my gaze, the night had thickened while I wasn't looking. Farther away, where the canal had shimmered, it soon rolled dark, opaque, its rivulets as secret as a dead man's dark hair. Under the birdsong that warm evening was a stillness you could feel, a full, rich stillness that added its urgency to my own.

The little door downstairs opened and then closed softly in that way Jan had. I stared as if falling through the tube of a telescope. I waited for him. Jan came into the room, came to me and held me hard around the shoulders. It felt as if he were forgiving me for something.

Later, lying in the dark, something came out.

I said, "Will you move in here with me now? Will you?"

"I guess I'll be taking my things out of Seekt's," he answered in the dark. "Shall we live together? What will your mother say?"

"It will be all right," I said. "Mother will be fine. We can have bigger windows put in one of these rooms for your painting."

"No painting, little flower," he said, very quietly.

"What?" I said.

After a while, Jan said in the dark, "Well, I tried to do it in prison—the first thing I thought of to do was to draw on the wall with some charcoal I found. I had an interesting idea and I was a little excited about it. But I couldn't do it. I tried several times, but it disgusted me. I found that it disgusted me. I didn't know why until, after sleeping one night, I woke up and realized why. I learned to paint from these people, I learned to paint for these people, and I have painted very little else but them."

"What people?" I asked.

"The ones who put me and my sister in prison, who make laws. People who run things. I did it for them. It's like I was their creature. It's what I always did. It's been my life and all I did since I left Seekt's protection, really. But with all that's happened, I can't do it any more. It disgusts me because they disgust me. I guess I am realizing I am different from them. I don't like them. My painting belongs too much to them, or to my trying to be in their world. I tried again in my studio at Seekt's last night and I couldn't even do a little memorial of Seekt. Nothing."

I was suddenly crying on his shoulder, and he comforted me until I went to sleep.

The morning wasn't very good either, because I had to tell him that he had to go and see the prins the next day. He understood, but of course he seemed pretty sour about it, and I feared that it made him identify me with that world. We didn't fight, but he rode away quite early and didn't tell me where he was going. I followed him down the stairs saying, "Will you have dinner with me tonight? Will you come back for dinner?" He smiled at me in an apologetic way, took my head and roughed my hair and pressed me to him. But I couldn't tell anything from his voice when he said, "I'll see you later."

That night was worse, mostly small talk and distance. The cooler it became, the more frightened I became. After he'd fallen asleep, I went downstairs to the gallery, pacing again on the moonlit black and white tiles, down the vista of tall glass doors, where Moenen had stood, where I had stood when I was a child the winter before. Then I had been lonely for a world that was yet to be. Now I was desperate for a world that was the only possible one for me and yet was vanishing. To get my mind off Jan, I worried about how many of Governor Iselin's financial meetings I would have to begin attending.

The next day, I wanted to be gone before Jan rode to the prins's palace. Before we parted we hugged just as if there were no difficulty between us, and I made him promise to come and tell me what happened. I rode to Seekt's house to see Katje. His gates were open and the yard was very neat. Matt was nowhere around and there was an impression of solitude. The door of the stairs up to quarters was shut and locked. I tied my horse, and walked up to the porch that overlooked the garden. There I saw an amazing sight. Far at the foot of the garden, past the lines of rose and rhododendron bushes, Katje was walking back and forth with my brother. They walked slowly along the hedge that bordered the field, deep in conversation. I walked down to them, past the lines of red-pink flower petals glistening in the clean morning light.

They turned to me with considered, thoughtful looks on their faces, almost sympathetically. They seemed very serious, waiting for me. When I had come near them, I realized that the situation was an awkward one.

"We're discussing business," Moenen said finally. He and Katje continued to stare at me.

"Well, I won't interrupt. Out for a ride. See you later." I strode up the lawn again. Mounting my horse, I wondered if someday I took a fancy to a goat, would Moenen chase after that, too?

That night, I waited in my rooms for Jan to return from the prins. I lighted one candle under the little round mirror. Soon Jan came in, almost silently. Then he was at my chair. In the candlelight I could see a startling, wistful expression on his face. And I could see love again. I could see what he felt for me showing in his face, as it used to.

"What happened?" I asked.

"Nothing, nothing," he said. He lifted me from the chair and kissed me once, then held me, feeling the muscles of my arms. He looked at me, examined me, as I had seen him examine paintings. Silently, he touched his hand along the features of my face, cheekbones, the curve of my chin. Then he closed my eyes and felt over them. He said, "I know I've been strange lately. I don't know what to do. But will you lie down with me? Lie with me for a while, I don't want to be alone."

I didn't know what he meant about being alone. Of course he wouldn't be alone. I left the candle to burn down, and we got into bed. I snuggled against him; I didn't know what else he wanted, and I didn't want to upset him, so I just tried to be warm. He lay there with his eyes open, so solemn.

"Tell me about the prins," I said. "Did he exact a price from your young flesh for his boon to you?"

"No," said Jan into the dark. "Hold me."

"Did he make you kiss him?" I persisted.

"No, no," Jan's voice said beside me. "We talked."

"Did he wait for you in the leafy ballroom?" I asked.

"Yes. What a terrible place. He asked me if I would paint a portrait of him, and I said that I could not. He said a royal commission was never refused, and he pressed me, so I explained that I could not paint, all the reasons why. He seemed to admire me, and started giving me compliments. He was so charming that before I knew it he had forced me to be intimate with him. And he wanted something. His eyes were hungry; I could see it.

"Then he asked me if I would lie down. He said all I would have to do was lie down. Then I got angry, and I said something like, 'I'm never going to lie down for any man,' or something like that, and he laughed at me. So I burst out with all these things; I paced up and down and poured out all the bitterness I've been feeling. And he listened. It felt good to be getting it out. Then he asked me how I would support myself if I did not paint, and I said I didn't know. He asked what would happen to my liaison with you if I didn't support myself and had nothing to do, and I became very confused. He worked on me, saying how at odds I was with things around here. And then he offered me something. He said I should go with a small expedition of his to the Antilles, tropical islands in the Americas."

My body stiffened so suddenly that my legs hurt. Jan went on.

"He said one ship was leaving next week, and that he would follow in a second ship soon after. It will be an

MY BROTHER'S IMAGE 155

exploring party, to last almost a year. He named a fantastic sum I would be paid if I would be the artist, and go with them to draw the animals and plants of the islands. He said he would not accept any answer I gave this afternoon, that he would expect my real answer anytime in the next three days. I just looked at him, and walked out. I could feel his strange eyes on me all the length of that ballroom.

"I couldn't leave you, Steen. Oh, I'm sorry I've been so bad the last few days. It'll be better." Then he was up against my shoulder, molding himself to my body, grasping me. "I couldn't leave you, not now."

I let him caress me, and settle himself against me. I patted him, so he would know it was all right. Just that he'd said he wouldn't leave was enough for that moment. I could sleep, secure with him. But I knew that wasn't the end of it.

I was good to him on purpose when we woke. I burned some breakfast for us and we ate heartily. He kept looking into my eyes. He had no errands or anything that morning, and seemed inclined to stay inside. So I went out and walked alone in our garden, then down the path that follows the canal. I tried to think, walking beside the wide, deep water. I tried to think. Two eels glided, silvery, just under the surface of the canal below me. I wondered if they would reach the sea. Feeling large and empty, like an empty shell, I looked into the far distance until it filled me. Then I was on my way to my horse.

I hardly saw the roads until I found myself passing the last of the horrible marshes, cantering down the lane between the rows of giant poplar trees. The sandy courtyard was as before, and, as before, the footman in blue was soon coming down the stairs to take my horse. Yes, the prins was in, he said. Up toward the vast sandstone facade, through the high doors, then a footman was conducting me along that long route that would end at the leafy ballroom.

The long walk, and two doors swung open to the sound of skittering leaves. He stood quite still, far down the parquet floor. He waited, silent, in that breathless gray velvet suit with the gold star on his chest. Nearing him, I bowed, then stood up and looked him in the eye.

"The answer is no," he said, looking into me. Panic flooded me from the top of my skull. "You can't come along. And it is for your own good. I don't say you will ever thank me for it, but it is better for you," he continued, his eyes into my eyes.

"It is *not!*" I shouted, growing red.

He said, "You see, Jan is going into a new world. He is going alone. You are from the old one. I know how you must dream of the warm nights on shipboard, and perhaps there would be those. But the old has soured for Jan, and sooner or later you would come between Jan and his life. It would be hell for you."

I stared at him, at the bald, wizened man with moist eyes.

"I think the sublime visits us," he continued, fucking me with his eyes now, "on its own terms, in its own time. To try to follow it, departing, or hold it, is to tear oneself to pieces."

"I want . . ." I said. "I want . . ."

"You want the world, boy," he said. "And that is not in my gift, the world."

I wanted to say I would fit my own ship and follow them, but I knew it would sound stupid.

"Just be glad," the prins said, "be grateful that you had it for a time. That can sometimes be enough."

"Enough?" I echoed. "Never. That's second best."

"It is your sacrifice, then," he said. "They told me, too, once . . ." The prins was musing now, sun on his bald dome, his young eyes darting down the length of the ballroom. "Somebody said, 'We will have this forever' and I knew I would not. I knew there would come the time when beauty's smile would not warm my lips any more, not mine. Then it is your sacrifice, waiting until the god turns his face to you again.

"On the day you walk out without him, into the day alone . . . it is such moments that you must live for, not the easy ones. It is in these moments that you break the golden image that is yourself, and distribute its treasure all over the world. For your own sake, because you are alone, you break your golden image, and the earth is filled with treasure for you."

MY BROTHER'S IMAGE

"But . . ." I was saying, head back, wetness brimming my eyes.

"So that if they ever ask you what it was to be a man, you see," the prins was saying, and I felt his finger scrape the tears where they brimmed over my cheeks, "you can tell them 'Oh, it was wonderful.'"

As I lowered my head, my tears spilled. I heard the rasping of dead leaves chasing one another over the vast floor behind me, and I turned and ran.

Jan was sitting by my windows, looking out at the evening. Bewildered giant. We were silent for a while, then he got up and leaned in the window bay, facing me. "I love you," he said.

"I know," I said.

"I don't want to go, Steen," he said.

"You have to. You know it's too good to say no," I said, the words absolutely dead. But his eyes had brightened, they had. I made the effort. "And besides, after you've sailed I can see the prins. Maybe I can persuade him to let me join the second ship," I said.

That was sufficient, and this was the moment when I knew the prins was right, for Jan said, "We could get brown together. We could live in a hut and run naked to the ocean."

"All right, then," I said. "You go tell the prins tomorrow. Don't tell him about me, because I'll work on him after you've sailed."

"What if the ships don't make it?" he said.

"Don't worry," I replied, "Dutch navigators are the best in the world."

The next days were full of Jan's departure. We went about town buying India goods—strong clothing, canvas for a tent, hides sewn together to contain water, strong shoes. He bought new materials for sketching and drawing. I bought him a marvelous kit that contained eating implements and a razor and a mirror. And he rode about saying his good-byes.

The evening before Jan was to sail, Peter and Christian came to dinner in the big dining room downstairs. I had sent a message to the see, inviting them, but I did not expect the companion they brought. As they rode up, there was a third figure riding manfully between them on a pony. It was little Cornelius. When I greeted him in the hall, he looked up at me as if I were the man in the moon. "We never played," he said to me.

"He wanted to see the one who saved him," Christian told me.

We all went in to dinner. I had had a lot of silver laid at our places, and there was candlelight. Jan talked about his trip, what it might be like on the ocean. He asked them how things were at the see, and what they were planning to do. Peter said his father had asked to see them, not him alone, but him and Christian together. Their plans would depend on whether there was a reconciliation at home. After the food was served, I noticed Cornelius was staring straight ahead of him, furiously, hands in his lap, while the food steamed in front of his face.

"What is it, Cornelius, why aren't you eating?" I asked.

He didn't respond except with a flicker of his eyes, looking very grave. I made a guess, and went to his place. I whispered in his ear, selected one of the forks, and put it in his hand. "Come on, now." He began to eat enormous mouthfuls, and my guests hid their smiles in the shadows of the candlelight. I asked Cornelius if he would like to stay with me for a while, and he seemed happy about that. So I had one of the rooms in my wing made ready for him, and after Peter and Christian left I went upstairs with him and got him settled in. He climbed into bed, and I pulled the covers up to his neck and sat with him for a while. I told him that he could live here, and get to know mother. His eyes got very big. I said that soon we could go to the country, a different place this time. I told him about the millpond and the tall trees around it, and about the great bird my brother once caught there when he was just a little older than Cornelius. Soon Cornelius was sleeping. I walked down the hall to my rooms, where Jan was waiting for me. He had lighted only the candle under the little circular mirror. I stood there a while, watching candlelight play on the shapes of his naked back, imagining tropical moons.

* * *

Next morning we rode down to the harbor in the carriage. While his bags were taken on board, he hugged me very hard, in plain view of all.

"Good-bye, my friend," I said, and he ran up the gangplank without saying anything. I think he was too agitated to speak. He took his place at the end of a line of crewmen then, earnest, at attention. I watched from the pier, where he could see me. As they pulled up the gangplank and drew in the anchor, the captain began a roll call of the ship's company. In the still, sunny morning I heard the names called and the answers shouted. Jan was the last in line, and as the ship began to move, gliding almost imperceptibly, I heard his name. I watched him standing straight and tall as he shouted, "Present!"

Roll call over, Jan went to the stern rail to watch me. I ran to the edge of the pier, and as the stern passed I stared up at him. "Steen," he shouted, and raised his arm to throw something. "Keep this till you see me!" He threw it as the ship glided by. The object glittered in the sun, flashing gold as it hurtled toward me. I reached up and snatched it from the air, his gold watch and chain. When I looked up to wave it at him, they had passed from view behind another ship.

Some days later, as I stood in our garden by the canal, I felt I was being observed. The feeling was so strong that I walked through the French doors into the gallery to check. Moenen stood by the open doors, and far down the gallery stood Katje. As I saw her on the black and white tiles wearing her black velvet dress, white lace at the neck, she was fixed like a doll in that shaft of sunlight. Moenen had been waiting for me, I could see. He wore his ice-blue silks.

"I have news," he said.

And I said, "Don't you mean 'We have news,' little brother?"

"Quick brother," Moenen said.

"You too," said I.

"No," Moenen replied, "we can't have the ceremony for months yet. But the papers are signed."

"Good girl," I said.

"Yes, she is," Moenen said, which left us looking into each other's eyes.

Katje's voice came down the gallery like a shot, breaking in: "All right, Steen?"

"Yes, ma'am," I shouted.

"Is it fair?" she shouted.

"I guess," I shouted.

Katje turned her back to us.

Then Moenen took my shoulders in his hands. By the bright light of that terrible spring, standing in the windows again, I looked at his face. I remember the curves of it as he drew close, his mouth and nose, the sunlight sparkling on his eyelashes. Ghosts of desire darted over his smooth, expectant features. Quickly, he inclined his head to kiss me.

Not so long ago—only months ago, all that. Now as I finish this a huge full moon has risen, red, crimson, at the edge of the ocean. Its bright crimson carpet ripples straight across the sea to me. The breeze has been steady all week, and the captain of this merchantman tells me we should drop anchor in the Antilles tomorrow. Then I will have to hurry because, you see, I'd like tomorrow's red moon to silhouette Jan as I climb over the last dune to see him running out of the night surf, tossing his wet hair in the wind, the moment before he looks up to discover I have come.